"WHAT—WHAT DID YOU DO THAT FOR?" RACHEL asked, her voice sounding low and husky and disoriented.

"The usual reasons. I wanted to." He paused, scanning her features, her mouth that still felt swollen from his kiss, her skin that tingled, as if she'd just gripped a jolt of pure electricity with both hands.

"And face it, Rachel darlin'," he added softly. "You wanted it too."

She opened her mouth to argue, to deny his words, but the truth pounded into her chest like a fist. He was right. Since the day she arrived she had been craving his kiss. The taste of him in her mouth, the touch of those hard, rough hands on her skin, the press of his body against hers.

She just hadn't been smart enough to figure that out until now.

"I don't . . ." She fought the urge to cover her suddenly burning face with her hands. Instead, she straightened her spine, lifted her chin, and forced herself to meet his gaze. "That is, it's probably not a smart idea for us to, um, engage in this sort of behavior again."

He nodded. "You're right about that. Truth is, though, I'm afraid I don't feel too smart when I'm around you."

WHAT ARE *LOVESWEPT* ROMANCES?

They are stories of true romance and touching emotion. We believe those two very important ingredients are constants in our highly sensual and very believable stories in the LOVE-SWEPT line. Our goal is to give you, the reader, stories of consistently high quality that may sometimes make you laugh, sometimes make you cry, but are always fresh and creative and contain many delightful surprises within their pages.

Most romance fans read an enormous number of books. Those they truly love, they keep. Others may be traded with friends and soon forgotten. We hope that each LOVESWEPT romance will be a treasure—a "keeper." We will always try to publish

LOVE STORIES YOU'LL NEVER FORGET
BY AUTHORS YOU'LL ALWAYS REMEMBER

The Editors

Loveswept® 862

FIREWORKS

RAEANNE THAYNE

BANTAM BOOKS
NEW YORK · TORONTO · LONDON · SYDNEY · AUCKLAND

FIREWORKS

A Bantam Book / December 1997

ISBN 0-553-44570-7

Published simultaneously in the United States and Canada

Bantam Books are published by Bantam Books, a division of Bantam Dou-
bleday Dell Publishing Group, Inc. Its trademark, consisting of the words
"Bantam Books" and the portrayal of a rooster, is Registered in U.S.
Patent and Trademark Office and in other countries. Marca Registrada.
Bantam Books, 1540 Broadway, New York, New York 10036.

PRINTED IN THE UNITED STATES OF AMERICA

OPM   10 9 8 7 6 5 4 3 2 1

To my parents, Elden and RaNae
Robinson, who gave me my love of
reading and my curiosity about how
things work. I love you both!

Special thanks to Blain Hamp for his
fire-fighting knowledge and for being
the brother my husband never had.

ONE

"Dad! She's here! She's here!"

Sam Wyatt turned his attention from the massive Engelmann spruce log he was working on, to see Noah barreling toward him, blond hair scrunched under a backward baseball cap and his face lit up like it was Christmas Eve.

"She's here! Did ya hear me, Dad?"

"I think they heard you over in Pinedale, son." Sam realized his hands had tightened on the drawknife, and he forced them to relax.

"Grandma Jo told me to come fetch you," Noah said, his voice high-pitched with excitement.

"She did, did she?" Sam carefully set aside the tool he used to hand-peel bark from the logs for the homes he built, then crossed to the hose attached to the side of the building.

"Yep." Noah grinned, flashing the gap he was so proud of in his bottom row of teeth. "She said to tell you to put a shirt on, too, or she'd skin you alive."

Sam paused in the middle of splashing icy water on his face to glance at his son. "Now that would be a trick, wouldn't it, since I'm twice as big as she is."

Noah giggled. "But Grandma Jo's quicker than spit. Zach said so, last week when she was tryin' to get him to take an icky-bleecky bath."

Sam smiled, despite the fact that all his attention was focused on the house and the woman whose presence there beckoned him like water draws cattle. Rachel. His children's aunt by marriage. The widow of his best friend, who had also been his late wife's brother. The woman who had been twisting his insides around since the day he met her.

Hell and damnation. Why couldn't she have stayed away another five years? Maybe then he'd have been ready to see her.

"Come *on*, Dad! I didn't even get to see what she brought me or nothin'. Grandma Jo made me run right down here to get you when we saw her car comin' up the road. Wait'll you see it! It's red and doesn't even have a roof on it! Maybe she'll let me and Zach ride in it while she's here. Think so, Dad? Dad?"

With a jolt, Sam realized that while he'd been standing there woolgathering about Rachel, the forgotten hose had been spraying onto his work boots. Precious, valuable water soaked with reckless abandon into the parched soil. He quickly drenched the towel he kept handy and turned off the spray.

Great. He had a million things to do before the snow flew thick and fierce in another few months: four houses in the final stage of construction, bidding on three more for work during the winter, his small herd of range cattle to round up.

The last thing he needed was Rachel Lawrence sauntering back into his life during his busiest time of the year. Rachel and her country-club clothes and her flashy convertible, who played havoc with his concentration without even trying.

"Dad? You comin' or not?"

"Go on ahead, son," Sam said, then cleared the gruffness from his voice. "Tell Grandma Jo and your brother I'll be up in a minute."

With a grin and wave, Noah headed back up to the house, skinny legs pumping. Sam watched him for a moment, then covered his face with the wet cloth and toweled off his chest and arms.

Why did she have to come back? Maybe he could have dealt with it if he'd had a few months to prepare, to convince himself what he'd experienced all those years ago had just been a natural reaction to a beautiful woman, not something dark and forbidden. But Josie had sprung it on him only a few hours earlier. One moment he'd been enjoying a forkful of her divine waffles, the next he'd been staring at her openmouthed, the waffles as tasty as cement chinking.

Somehow he'd managed to choke them down. "Rachel? Coming *here?*"

At least Josie had had the grace to look uncomfortable. Her gaze had dropped back to the waffle iron and she'd fidgeted just like one of the boys after they brought home a less-than-perfect report card.

"I didn't figure you'd mind, Sam," she said. "You know we got plenty of room around here."

He continued to stare until Jo's expression grew fierce. "She's as much my family as you are, young man. With Hannah and Matt both gone now, the people they married and your boys are about all I have left." She paused, then swiped a strand of steel-gray hair from her face with a thin hand. " 'Sides, I miss her, and so do those boys of yours."

True enough. After Josie told them Rachel was coming, Noah and Zach talked of nothing else all morning, just as they would become consumed with excitement whenever their aunt Rachel deigned to send a package from her daddy's Santa Barbara estate.

He'd never been able to figure out the bond between them. Zach had been only three when she'd married Matt and moved there, but he'd followed her around like a puppy on a bone. And Noah probably didn't even remember what she looked like, since he hadn't even been out of diapers when she'd left Whiskey Creek for good.

Sam remembered, though. In excruciating detail. He had a quick mental picture of impossibly long legs, big doelike gray eyes, and hair the same deep, pure auburn that glowed inside the heart of a burning log. He remembered vividly the way she used to tuck that hair behind her ear when she was concentrating on something and the way her smile would creep out of nowhere.

And the way she looked at Matt as if the whole world would stop spinning if he wasn't around.

Of course, that was until she had shocked them all by leaving that grim day five years ago, only to find herself a widow before she could get any farther than Jackson Hole.

Sam frowned. He remembered too much about her, that was for damn sure. And just when his mental picture of her had begun to fade—when he thought he'd found some measure of peace from it—she had to sneak her long legs and her doe eyes and that hair back into his life.

He sighed and shrugged into his T-shirt. Nothing he could do about it except go up to the house to greet her, even though all his better instincts were hollering at him to run away as fast as he could.

She shouldn't have come, Rachel thought, words she'd repeated at least a hundred times during the hot, dusty drive from Jackson Hole.

She should have just flown out for her conference, then headed back to California without letting a soul in town know she was in Wyoming. Even better, she should have bypassed the conference altogether and had her assistant at the William J. Lawrence Foundation come in her stead.

If she'd been thinking at all, she would have realized Josie was likely to insist she come to Whiskey Creek the minute she found out Rachel had traveled east of the Sierra Nevadas. Of course, she hadn't been thinking. Not when she agreed to attend the conference in the first place and not when she happened to let slip to Josie in one of their infrequent phone calls that she would be in Wyoming.

Ever since learning the annual conference would be

held in Jackson Hole—just an hour from the Wind River Mountain Range and the town of Whiskey Creek—she'd been unable to escape the memories, unable to shake the pain and the guilt that still followed her like phantom shadows, even five years after Matt's death.

Those five years had wrought few changes in the place, she thought now. The mountains still loomed in the background, primeval and menacing. Even though it was the middle of the driest, hottest August the West had seen in years, snow still glistened on their glacial peaks.

She knew from bitter experience that in another few months, new snow would coat the whole Whiskey Creek valley several feet thick, freezing out whatever sparks of life somehow managed to find a foothold in the desolate place.

The rented BMW bounced on a rut in the dirt road as she passed underneath a massive log arch. Well, a few things were new, she amended, glancing at the arch in her rearview mirror. Someone had hewn out the words "Whiskey Creek Log Homes" and painted the letters green, in contrast with the rich honey color of the logs. Sam, probably, she thought. Jo had told her his business was doing well, that he was building homes as far away as Bozeman.

Any thought of Sam and his business was wrenched from her mind when Rachel rounded the last curve of the hilly road to the old homestead. She stared and braked the car in a cloud of dust.

Okay, so a great deal had changed on the Elkhorn. A rambling two-story log home with gabled windows and a wide front porch had sprung up in the five years since she'd been there, and the old tumbledown barn sparkled in the harsh sun with a fresh coat of scarlet paint.

Another careful, sweeping glance at the cluster of outbuildings completed the picture for her. She could find absolutely no sign of the old ranch house and the little foreman's cabin, with its splintery wood floors and homespun curtains, where she and Matt had lived during their painfully short marriage.

Matt.

Rachel leaned back against the seat of the car and closed her eyes, seeing his face behind her eyelids, young and strong and full of a deep, abiding love of life. The fluttering panic began in the center of her chest and rippled through the rest of her.

She couldn't do this. She didn't have the strength to face his family after all that had gone between them. It was so much easier—safer—to stay in her carefully cushioned world in Santa Barbara. To pretend to herself and to those who knew her that her brief time here had never happened.

She opened her eyes in time to see two little figures leaning on the wide porch railing of the house, waving wildly. Despite her turmoil, a breathless laugh escaped her at the sight of Zach and Noah racing down to the gravel driveway to wait for her.

They were the reason she was there, the only thing that could have induced her to break her vow never to return to Whiskey Creek—those two motherless boys she had loved from the moment she'd held them, when

Matt had dragged her to his family's ranch after their whirlwind courtship.

Before she could talk herself out of it, Rachel put the car in gear and drove the remaining distance to the house. She stopped the little rental, and with hands that shook only slightly, clipped back the stray strands of hair that had flown loose during the drive from Jackson.

With one last deep, fortifying breath, she stepped out of the car.

"Aunt Rachel! Aunt Rachel!" The two boys flung themselves at her, squeezing her so tightly she had to back against the car for support. Her arms instinctively went around them and she gathered them close. A wave of emotion, powerful and strong, crashed through her, and she couldn't speak for the lump in her throat.

Even though she hated Whiskey Creek and everything it represented in her life, she loved these two dear little boys with all her heart.

Over the years, she'd seen pictures and even the occasional videotape that Jo was kind enough to send her. They'd traded letters and phone calls and Christmas presents. But nothing matched the bittersweet joy of holding them in her arms.

"Aunt Rachel! I thought you'd never get here! I've missed you so much!"

"Well, I'm here now." She smiled in response to Noah's gap-toothed grin, though she felt her eyes moisten. "I've missed you, too, sweetheart. My word, Noah. You're all grown up! And Zach. Are you shaving yet?" she teased the older boy, who was nine.

A blush coated his cheekbones, and he pulled away

and scratched his dark blond hair, then stuck his hands in his back pockets. "Nah. I told Dad I'm ready, but he's probably gonna make me wait at least 'til I'm twelve. Stupid, huh?"

"What'd you bring me?" Noah asked eagerly, craning his neck to see the packages in the backseat of the car.

She smiled, fighting the urge to smooth his darling blond cowlick. "Oh, this and that. I suppose you'll just have to wait and see, won't you?"

"Boys!" a familiar sharp voice interjected. "Quit maulin' your aunt and let her catch her breath."

Rachel glanced to the porch where Matt's mother waited, arms folded across her skinny chest and a wary, but not unwelcoming, light in her flashing dark eyes.

Rachel straightened, her arms falling from Noah. "Hello, Josie."

" 'Bout time you decided to show your face around here again, don't you think?"

Rachel couldn't stop the heat that rushed to her face or the guilt curling through her. Jo knew perfectly well why she'd stayed away so long. She probably also knew Rachel would rather be anywhere else on earth than right there, except for these two adorable boys, with their freckled noses and broad, elated smiles.

"Five years is an awful long time to stay away from your family," Jo went on.

Despite her inward flinch, Rachel met the older woman's gaze head-on. "You're right. It is."

Jo walked down the steps and studied her for a few more moments, then wiped her hands on her apron.

"Well, you're here now. That's the important thing, I guess. Come over and give an old woman a hug."

Rachel obeyed and pressed her cheek against Jo's weathered face. She closed her eyes for a moment. The last time they'd embraced had been before she left, when both of them had believed they'd likely never see each other again.

Jo was the first to pull away. "How long can you stay?"

"I need to be back Monday—" she began, when a flurry of movement near the corner of the house distracted her. She knew it was Sam before she even turned her head. A sense of impending danger had warned her. She drew in a calming breath and turned to face him.

"Sam."

It was all she could force from a mouth suddenly dry. He was the one she dreaded seeing: Sam, who had been her husband's best friend and who now despised her. With good reason.

"Rachel." His gaze was stony, cold, as she'd expected. Once those eyes—bluer than the bluest Wyoming sky—had looked at her with if not respect, then with at least a grudging acceptance.

Now they gleamed with suspicion in a rugged, tanned face. His dark hair, falling nearly to the curve in the back where his neck met his shoulder, rippled in the hot wind and three droplets of water clung to the lean angle of his jaw.

He was bigger than she remembered, thick and strong and undeniably male, with wide shoulders barely fitting inside a worn navy T-shirt.

"See, Dad, I told you she had a cool car," Noah said, breaking the sudden, awkward silence, and Sam turned to look at it.

"Nice," he said, his tone impassive. "Wouldn't do you much good in the wintertime around here, though. You need something a little more solid when the going gets tough."

Rachel wasn't stupid enough to think he was talking about the car. She vividly remembered his words after Matt's funeral when she'd told him she was leaving, returning to Santa Barbara.

"You never belonged here anyway. Matt was a fool to think you did."

Her cheeks burned and her stomach twisted with nerves. For an instant, the pines around the house seemed to dip and sway, and she reached a hand behind her for balance, for the security of the rental car.

She hadn't eaten anything since lunchtime the previous day, she suddenly realized. She'd been too nervous to eat. Or sleep, for that matter. Lack of food and sleep, combined with the drive out there in the steady heat, must be causing her dizziness. It certainly couldn't have anything to do with Sam.

"You feelin' okay?" Jo demanded. "You're lookin' a mite peaked."

"I . . . yes. I'm fine."

"Well, we certainly don't have to stand out here in this sun yammerin'," Jo said. "Sam, don't just stand there. Bring her bags in, why don't ya?"

Before she could object, Sam obediently reached into the backseat where she'd stowed her luggage.

Rachel straightened away from the car. "But . . .

Oh, no. I'm not staying." She reached across to take them from Sam, and her fingers accidentally brushed against his big, rough hands. They fumbled over the bags briefly until she jerked them away.

"But Aunt Rachel! You said." Noah looked stunned at first, then on the verge of tears. "You said you could stay until Monday. You said!"

All thought of her suitcases and the odd, arcing spark she'd felt when she touched Sam flew away at the little boy's anguish. She knelt to his level, aching at the tears that shimmered in Noah's vivid blue eyes, so much like his father's.

"Oh, sweetheart. I meant I'd stay in Whiskey Creek, not here at the Elkhorn. I made reservations at that bed and breakfast in town. I wouldn't want to impose on you here."

"Don't be silly," Jo said brusquely. "You can just call 'em and break your reservation. We got plenty of room, and we can fix you breakfast just as well here. Might not be as fancy as what you'd find there, but it'll stick to your ribs. You'll stay here and that's the end of the discussion. Isn't that right, Sam?"

He didn't want her there. She knew it perfectly well, could see it in his frown, in his stiff posture, in his eyes that could freeze out the entire state of Wyoming when he wanted them to. He couldn't have made it more clear. Still, the stubborn man just nodded.

"Sure," he drawled. "Plenty of room."

"Please, Aunt Rachel." Zach added his voice to the others and it was that one she listened to most.

She adored Noah, with his pure, childlike enthusiasm, but Zach was the only one besides Matt who had freely accepted her presence when she lived there. He had showered her with all the unconditional love in his little heart. She owed him at least this much.

She nodded. "All right. If you're sure I'm not intruding."

"Don't be silly," Jo said. "You're family. I'll have lunch on in an hour. Meantime, Sam can take your things to the guest room so you can freshen up. Boys, you help me set the table."

"Aw, Grandma," they started to argue.

"That'll be enough of that," she said sternly. "Hop to it."

With the finesse of a cattle driver, Jo ushered them up the porch steps and into the house, leaving Rachel and Sam standing alone by the car. Without a word, he reached down and hefted her cases effortlessly.

"I can manage," she told him. "I'm sure you have things you need to be doing."

He ignored her. "Do you want that other bag back there too?"

She nodded, and he lifted it out and led the way into the house. Before he headed up the curving, half-log stairway, she had a quick impression of hunter-green carpet and homey, comfortable furnishings, a few of which she recognized from the old place.

She followed Sam up the stairs, trying fiercely not to notice how broad his shoulders were in the faded shirt. Why on earth was she even aware of something like that? Like how his muscles barely flexed carrying her heavy bags and how his hair curled slightly at the ends. He smelled of the earth. Like pine shavings and honest sweat.

Rachel flushed and jerked her mind away from such thoughts. What was the matter with her? This was *Sam*, for heaven's sake. She had no more business noticing those kinds of things about him than she had being back in Whiskey Creek.

The silence stretched between them, uncomfortably long, as they reached the top of the stairs and he led her along the balcony ringing the great room below. Uneasy, she gripped the handrail, smooth as polished stone under her fingers, as if it were a lifeline.

Finally, she couldn't stand it anymore as the instinct to make polite conversation—drilled into her by the best boarding schools money could buy—fought its way to the surface.

"You've made a lovely home here," she said.

He gave a half-turn and studied her out of hooded, wary eyes. "Thanks."

"Did you do all the work yourself?"

"Yeah. Most of it."

Determined to make him answer in more than monosyllables, she tried again. "I had no idea you were so skilled."

"It's construction work, Rachel. Not exactly quantum physics."

They had reached a doorway—the guest bedroom, she assumed—and he thrust open the door and carried her bags inside. Soft grays and blues in the carpet and bedding created a pleasing contrast to the warm, mellowed pine.

"It's beautiful, Sam," she said sincerely. "I can see you've worked hard on the place. How have you possibly had time to do so much around here, between the ranch and starting this log home business and fighting fires?"

He didn't meet her gaze, just plopped the suitcases onto the floor near the wide log bed. "I don't fight fires anymore," he said, his voice clipped. "Haven't done it for five years now."

For an instant, shock scrambled her thoughts. Five years. When Matt had died while the two of them had been fighting a wind-whipped timber fire near Pinedale. Rachel felt that jittery, panicky feeling swell in her chest again at the memories.

Sam, like her husband, had lived and breathed firefighting. Even before he had married Matt's sister, Hannah, the two men had shared a deep, lasting bond, forged in heat and flames and the adrenaline rush of battling together against the elements.

Rachel had hated that bond as much as she'd hated this place.

She quickly tried to gather her composure around her again. "I see," she said quietly.

"Do you?"

The bitterness in his voice shredded what little remained of her careful calm. Maybe it was because of the stress of coming back, or the crushing heat of the day, or the nausea that still roiled in her stomach from the long, jarring drive out there, but for the first time in years, she felt her emotions slip away from her.

"Look, Sam, I know how you feel about me," she bit out. "You think I'm spoiled and selfish. Oh, yes, let's not forget manipulative."

He stared. "I never called you any of those things."

"Maybe not in so many words, but that's what you meant after Matt's funeral, isn't it?"

He looked as if he wanted to deny it, but he clamped his lips together in a tight line.

Hot, aching emotions clogged her throat. She swallowed them down and hid behind anger. "Well, I am so sorry to inflict my spoiled, selfish, manipulative self on your life again. But I'm only going to be here for two days. Two lousy days. Can't we at least try to be civilized for the sake of the boys?"

"I'm just a Wyoming cowboy, Rachel, not one of your slick society friends. Our definitions of civilized are probably as far apart as caviar and Rocky Mountain oysters."

"I'm here to see the boys and Jo and that's it," she snapped. "If you don't want me here, I'll say good-bye right now, hop into my flimsy little car, and not look back. But you'll have to explain to your two sons why you can't stand to have me around. So either lighten up or—or go *stuff* your Rocky Mountain oysters."

After her impassioned speech, he studied her for a moment out of those crystal blue eyes; then, without warning, he chuckled. It started deep in his chest and expanded, full and rich, easing into just about every corner of the room.

Rachel stared at him, at the sun-etched furrows at the corners of his eyes, at the way his firm, full lips widened with his smile, at the way his teeth gleamed in the light from the wide bank of windows.

"What's so darn funny?" she finally growled.

"You ever tried Rocky Mountain oysters?"

"No."

"Well, take it from me, they taste like hell. I don't imagine stuffing 'em would make 'em taste much better. I could ask Josie to fix you up a batch, if you want, though. For company and all."

Despite herself, Rachel felt an answering smile take over her mouth before she could hold it back. "You always did know how to yank my chain," she murmured.

"Yeah, if there's one thing I'm good at, it's yanking chains." He gave a lopsided grin, then reached out to tug a lock of her hair that had again slipped free.

She stiffened as his hard, rough hand fell away from her face. To her relief, he didn't appear to notice as he turned and walked out the door, still laughing.

For a moment, she couldn't move, frozen except for the trembling in her knees. Then she crossed to the door and closed it carefully behind him, as if it were made of the finest spun glass and would shatter into tiny pieces if she barely touched it. Without even bothering to take off her shoes, she flopped onto the bed and stared up at the sloping half-logs in the ceiling.

She didn't know what she was doing there, how she would deal with Sam, who could make her want to yell one minute and laugh the next. She also didn't know if she had the strength to face her past, the ghosts that seemed to surround her.

She did know one thing, though. She should never have come back.

TWO

Loud whispers dragged Rachel out of the exhausted sleep she had slipped into. She opened her eyes to find two impatient-looking young men in the doorway peeking in on her.

"You think she's asleep or just fakin'?"

"Noah, you're such a dummy," Zach said. " 'Course she's asleep. Why would she want to fake it?"

"You're the big dummy. Maybe she's just teasin'."

"Nah. Aunt Rachel wouldn't play tricks on us," the older boy said loyally.

She decided she had better speak before they started slugging it out. "Hi, guys." The words came out gruff and she cleared her throat. "How long have I been asleep?"

"See," Zach said with the superior air of a smug older brother. "Told you she wasn't fakin'."

"I'm sorry," she said, pulling herself to a sitting position. "I didn't mean to crash on you guys. It's—it's been a long week." She hadn't had more than a few hours of sleep a night, consumed with the knowledge that she was returning.

"It's okay, Aunt Rachel," Zach assured her. "It hasn't even been an hour. We didn't mean to bug you. Grandma Jo sent us up to check on you, to see if you're ready for lunch. If you want to go back to sleep, we can tell her you'll eat later."

"No. I don't want to sleep, I want to be with you two as long as I can. Let me wash up and I'll be right down."

With luck, their father would be gone by the time she made it downstairs, Rachel thought, as they closed the door behind them.

Sam glanced up from his sandwich—roast beef piled on thick homemade bread—to see the boys thundering down the stairs. "Walk," he ordered them. "You keep racing around here like that and one of you is going to end up with a broken neck."

His boys just grinned at the familiar admonishment, though they tried to moderate their pace to a trot.

"Rachel's coming down," Zach informed them. "She just fell asleep."

Sam tried not to picture her warm and tousled from sleep, her hair loose and drifting across her face, that skin rosy and soft—

He took a gulp of ice water and slid his chair back from the table just as the boys jumped into their seats.

"Guess I'd better get back to work," he told Josie. She glanced up from the lettuce she was shredding for a salad, surprise in her eyes. "Now? You can't even stay five minutes to be civil to Rachel?"

"Where did everybody suddenly get this crazy idea I was civil?" He frowned while he carried his plate to the sink, rinsed it, and stuck it in the dishwasher.

"Beats me, the way you been actin' today," Josie said tartly. "If I didn't know better, I'd say you were . . ." She paused, and he could feel her sharp gaze boring through his shoulder blades.

"You'd say I was what?" He couldn't keep the belligerence out of his tone.

"Oh, never mind. Just a harebrained old woman's fancies," she muttered.

Josie just didn't know how to mind her own business, he thought. He loved her like the mother he'd never known, and he didn't know what he would have done on his own with two needy, bewildered boys after the shock of Hannah's sudden death, if it hadn't been for Hannah's mother.

Josie had picked him up from the hell he'd been living in, brushed him off, and kicked him in the seat until he realized he might be able to go on after all. He owed her, and it was a debt he knew he'd be a long time repaying.

Still, there were plenty of times he wanted to wring her skinny little neck. He shook his head and pulled a soft drink out of the refrigerator to take down to the barn with him for later, then grabbed his hat off the rack by the door.

"Sam!"

Her impatient voice halted him, and he stuck his head back through the doorway. "Yeah?"

"I thought it might be nice to take Rachel into town tonight, let her see some of the folks she knew when she was here. Maybe we could even have dinner at R.J.'s so I don't have to wear my back out fixin' somethin', for a change."

"Yes!" Noah and Zach high-fived each other, thrilled at the rare chance to eat out.

Sam studied her for a moment, then nodded. "You do that. The boys will enjoy it."

"What about you? You don't want to come with us?"

He'd rather have that half-ton log he was working on dropped on his bare toes.

"I've got to finish this McMullin project. With us still shorthanded, I could use all the time I can find."

"Sam Wyatt. You can get away from those blasted logs for five minutes to take your family to dinner."

He could, he admitted. He just didn't want to. He'd be better off staying as far away from Rachel Lawrence as possible.

"Come on, Dad. It wouldn't be half as much fun without you there."

"What wouldn't be half as much fun without your dad there?"

They all turned as Rachel entered the kitchen. She'd piled her hair into some kind of twisty hairdo, he noticed, and she'd put on shorts and a T-shirt the color of apricots just before they fell from the tree. She looked fresh and cool. Delectable.

Damn her.

"I thought we could drive into Whiskey Creek for dinner at R.J.'s." Jo smiled at Rachel, oblivious to his turmoil, to the sudden ache pulsing through him. "It would get me out of this kitchen and give you a chance to see some of the folks in town."

Interesting, Sam thought, noting the change in Rachel's expression. Why should the idea of R.J.'s make her actually pale?

"I . . . That would be nice," she said. Somehow he knew she was lying, although her face once again had that serene, composed look to it.

"Sam here says he doesn't have time to come with us," Jo went on, "and we're trying to talk him into it."

"Oh?"

"It's my busy season," he said, fingering the brim of his sweat-stained cowboy hat. As soon as the words slipped out, he could have kicked himself. He didn't need to explain anything to her. Not one single thing.

"Oh, in that case, I wouldn't want to keep you from your work." The relief was plain in her gray eyes. She didn't want him there any more than he wanted to go, he realized. For some reason, that knowledge annoyed him.

"I suppose I could spare one evening," he said before he thought it through. "For family and all."

"Really, Sam." Her voice was cool. "I'm sure we can manage fine without you. I wouldn't want to be a bother."

You're already a bother, lady, he thought, but wisely refrained from making the comment, what with Josie and the boys avidly watching the exchange. "If I'm not back by six, Jo, send one of the boys down to fetch me so I can shower and change."

Without risking another look at Rachel, he shoved

the hat on against the harsh glare of the sun and pushed open the screen door, wondering what the hell he'd just gotten himself into.

The door slammed shut behind him as loud as a gunshot, and Rachel jerked in her chair. Luckily, Jo had already turned back to the salad and the boys were too excited at the coming outing to notice.

How had she completely lost control of this whole situation? she wondered. The absolute last thing she wanted to do was spend an evening in such proximity to Sam, trying to pretend for Jo's and the boys' sakes she didn't feel his antagonism, the hostility that radiated from him like heat waves on an August sidewalk. Especially not in Whiskey Creek, where the residents had closed their minds and ranks against her from the moment she'd come there with Matt.

She'd wanted so desperately to belong, to be accepted into their close-knit community. But she'd been the proverbial fish out of water. Whiskey Creek was worlds away from her father's Santa Barbara estate, with its acres of manicured lawns and unobtrusive servants and excruciatingly polite inhabitants.

She'd tried for months to fit in, although she had to admit she hadn't tried very hard.

She hadn't known the first thing about the topics that interested most of the people in Whiskey Creek: crop rotations and beef futures and the latest irrigation systems.

When she is not well-informed on a topic, a young lady refrains from commenting, Rachel had been taught throughout her childhood. She'd spent her nine months in Wyoming refraining from commenting on much of anything, and the people of Whiskey Creek had taken her shyness for icy disdain. She'd felt it in their stares and she'd sensed it in the way the women would stop talking when she walked into the grocery store in town.

At first, she hadn't let it bother her, so wrapped up in Matt and the joy she found with him to let anything intrude in their perfect world. Then the fire season had hit with a vengeance and he'd gone to the latest hot spot, leaving her to cope with it all alone.

She'd been an outsider. At no time had she felt it more keenly than at Matt's funeral, when they had all watched her with barely concealed animosity. He had belonged, had been one of them in a way she could never be.

"Aunt Rachel?"

She roused herself from her grim thoughts to see the boys watching her with twin worried expressions on their faces. "I'm sorry. Did you say something?"

Noah still looked concerned. "Grandma Jo asked you three times what kind of gunk you want on your salad."

"That gunk is called dressing, no-brain," Zach said.

Rachel managed a smile. "Sorry, Jo. I'll have whatever's handy."

What did it matter? She wouldn't be able to taste it, anyway, not with her stomach twisted into knots at the idea of facing the people of Whiskey Creek again.

The boys didn't give her time to dwell on it, though. As soon as she'd eaten, she caved in to their entreaties and showed them the gifts she'd brought them—new GameBoys with several cartridges apiece, two new basketballs, and a couple of fancy flashlights.

After they'd played for a while with their new things, they dragged her outside to show her around the ranch. She didn't have the heart to tell them that during the time she was married to Matt, she saw more than she'd cared to of the old place.

She feigned enthusiasm when they showed her the chickens and Noah's cat Nuisance and the small pond out back that Sam had stocked with trout for the boys to catch. Gradually the enthusiasm became real, and she smiled with the innocent pleasure of it as she perched on the grassy bank of the pond and watched them practice skipping rocks. They were terrific boys. It couldn't have been easy for Sam on his own all these years.

Hannah had been killed in a car accident the winter before Rachel had moved there with Matt, so Sam had been alone with the boys far longer than he'd been married. Jo helped him, of course, but from what she could gather, Sam still did the bulk of the parenting on his own. It was obvious from the way the boys were turning out that he was managing just fine.

She watched Noah lie on his belly on the bank to look more closely at something in the water, and amended her thoughts. Better than fine. The boys had a marvelous childhood. Filled with laughter and rough-housing and the attention of an obviously devoted father. Even if Sam had had the means, she knew he would never send his children to any boarding school, no matter how exclusive.

Rachel stopped the direction of her thoughts,

ashamed of her self-pity. She hadn't had a bad child-hood. Just a carefully structured one. Was it any wonder she'd rebelled so thoroughly at the first opportunity by falling headlong in love with someone as completely unsuitable as Matt?

"Let's go see the horses." Noah, easily distracted, jumped to his feet and rushed over to her. "I've got my own pony, Aunt Rachel. His name's Petey. I picked it myself."

She smiled. "Petey's a great name for a pony."

"I know." Noah grinned that gap-toothed grin, and she wanted to grab him tight and squeeze. "Zach and Dad both have horses and we keep one for Grandma Jo to ride, but she never does. Zach's horse is named Pep and Dad's is Cap'n. I rode him once, too, 'cept he bucked me right off and Dad got madder than blazes at me. Boy, did he yell."

"You weren't supposed to be riding him, that's why," Zach said.

"Well, Dad didn't need to yell at me."

The boys continued their lighthearted bickering as they led the way along the split-rail fence back to the ranch. They had nearly reached the barn when she realized how close they'd come to where Sam worked.

She could see him, shirtless and in faded jeans, his muscles rippling as he used both hands to work some sort of sharp tool along the wood's surface so that the bark flaked away. Tanned and lean, he moved in a steady, hypnotizing rhythm.

Rachel stopped abruptly. A tingling awareness began in the center of her stomach and fluttered out until she felt it in her toes, in her fingertips. It wasn't a pleasant feeling at all, more like a thousand needle-pricks of sensation, as if her nerve endings had been frozen for years and were beginning the slow, painful process of thawing.

He paused his movements long enough to take the back of his leather-gloved hand and wipe away the beads of sweat she could see glistening on his forehead. Somehow he must have sensed her scrutiny, because he glanced up. His gaze met hers and held it for long seconds while the boys tugged impatiently on her hands.

Rachel shook her head to clear it and broke the eye contact with Sam. She could feel her face flush from more than the scorching heat, and would have pressed her hands to it if not for the boys tightly clinging to them.

She needed to get out more, she thought, horrified at the sensations still whipping through her.

Maybe if she saw someone besides the safe, comfortable men she'd known since childhood—the kind of men she tended to gravitate to in Santa Barbara—she wouldn't be so thrown at the sight of a man who was so unabashedly, intrinsically male. That was the only reason Sam was affecting her like this. It had to be. He was rough-edged and rugged, neither safe nor comfortable. Different from what she was used to. And completely off-limits.

"You see him, Aunt Rachel? Isn't he a beaut?"

For several seconds, she blinked at Noah, until she realized he was pointing to a buckskin pony grazing in the pasture, his long tail nearly reaching the grass.

"That's Petey," Noah said proudly.

"Yes," she said, and her voice cracked on the word. She cleared her throat. "He's beautiful."

"Let's go for a ride," Zach suggested. "I bet you could ride Grandma Jo's horse, Fanny. She's kinda slow but Dad says she's real sweet."

"Good idea," Rachel said. Anything to put distance between Sam and her absurd reaction to him.

As Sam had expected, dinner was a stilted affair, at least between Rachel and him. Josie and the boys didn't seem to notice the silences, the tension that vibrated in the air. Jo was abnormally quiet, but the boys chattered on about everything under the sun, about the heat, about school starting in less than a month, about their Little League baseball season.

Rachel, in a denim skirt and white lacy blouse, smiled at the boys and watched them with soft affection in her eyes, but whenever she looked away from them, her expression closed up again like Whiskey Creek on a Sunday.

He leaned back in the booth and watched her out of the corner of his eyes. She looked miserable, he realized. Again, that curiosity sneaked across his mind. What would cool, self-assured Rachel Lawrence possibly have to be miserable about in a place like R.J.'s?

With her hoity-toity background, she probably thought it was the worst kind of dive. He frowned, immediately on the defensive. R.J.'s certainly wasn't fancy, with its vinyl booths, motley paneling, and worn gray-speckled tabletops. But the food was hot and filling, and folks from as far away as Star Valley flocked there.

In wild and woolly Wyoming—where cattle outnumbered people by a long shot—just about any place where you could run into other people became a popular destination to meet and swap stories.

Maybe that was the very thing she didn't like about it. The people. Rachel had never quite fit in with folks around Whiskey Creek. She did fine out at the ranch, but bring her into town and she seemed to become as unapproachable as a porcupine, to put on a haughty air that kept anybody from trying to get close to her.

"Dad, can we put a quarter in the jukebox?"

He shrugged his thoughts away and fished a coin out of the pocket of his best jeans. With a flip, he tossed the quarter to a grinning Zach, who palmed it and slid out of the booth.

"Tell him he has to let me pick one of the songs!" Noah said.

"Let your brother have a turn."

Zach groaned but waited for Noah, then the two of them raced to the jukebox. Jo stood up as soon as they left.

"There's Polly Naylor over there having dinner with her daughter. Think I'll go say hello," she said, before heading toward a table on the other side of the café, leaving him and Rachel alone in the booth.

She seemed tired, Sam thought, watching Josie go. Not her usual affable self. He shifted his attention back to Rachel, who was fussing with the edge of her paper place mat. Everybody was acting strange that night, out of character. Rachel Lawrence simply wasn't the fidgety type.

"So. Is it like you remembered?" he finally asked, when the silence became uncomfortable.

She gave him a startled look. "Wh-What?"

"R.J.'s. I don't think it's changed much since you were here. Maybe a few new songs in the jukebox, but that's about it."

She paused, weighing her words in that careful way of hers. "You know, I feel as if I've tumbled through some kind of time warp. I think those people at the counter were sitting on exactly those same stools when I was here last. The menu is the same, people seem to be dressed in the very same clothes. Even their conversations sound the same."

"I guess some folks stick with what works."

Rachel studied his features, to see if there was some hidden, censorious message there, some undertone of accusation for her actions five years earlier. She couldn't read anything at all.

"I guess they do." Too late, when she could do nothing to snatch it back, she heard the trace of sorrow, of guilt, in her voice. Both of them knew she was not one of those people. Hadn't she proved it when she'd foolishly, selfishly, run out on Matt?

To her shock, Sam reached out a big, callused hand and placed it on her fists, clenched tightly together on the worn tabletop.

"I didn't mean anything by that. Sorry you took it wrong."

She slipped her hands away from him, from his heat and hardness, and hid them under the table so he wouldn't see their trembling. "It could have been what you meant, though. Right? It's nothing less than the truth. I'm not one of those people who sticks with what works."

He started to reply, but the boys gleefully returned to the booth before he could, while a honky-tonk Garth Brooks song suddenly rumbled out of the neon jukebox.

"I picked that one," Noah said, beaming with pride. "Zach picked a drippy, mushy one just 'cause Merilee Hansen's here." His mouth twisted with disgust and he made a gagging motion with his finger. "He sat with her on the bus every day during the last week of school. Gross, huh?"

His older brother's cheeks turned pink and he punched Noah in the shoulder.

Desperately grateful for their presence to break the tension between her and Sam, she smiled. "One of these days, young man, you might not think it's so gross."

He scrunched up his face as if she'd told him one day he'd enjoy eating frog intestines, and Rachel and Sam both laughed.

Jo returned just as the waitress delivered their food, and Rachel was content to listen to the affectionate banter of Sam and the boys. She'd missed this in California, she thought. She and her father seldom dined together because of their different schedules, so she often ate by herself while she pored over grant applications and the trust's paperwork. When she went out, it was usually social affairs, and she'd forgotten how comfortable a family dinner could be.

The second of their jukebox selections ended while they were still eating, and when no one else in the diner seemed compelled to pick another one, Noah decided he wanted to. This time the boys dragged Rachel with them to help them choose.

"I'm not very good at this sort of thing, guys," she told them with a laugh. "I'm afraid I'm not very current with today's music scene."

"Doesn't matter," Noah said. "I'll show you which one to pick."

They were dithering between a country tune and an old Beach Boys song when the bells above the door chimed.

"Rachel? Rachel Carson, is that you?"

She turned, disoriented at the sound of her married name, the first time she'd heard it in years, and followed the voice to a dark-haired woman holding a toddler in her arms. Andie McPhee, the only woman besides Josie she had considered a friend in Whiskey Creek, shrieked with delight and nearly dropped the giggling child. "It is you! I can't believe it!"

Rachel was immediately engulfed in a tight hug, child and all.

"How long has it been?" Andie went on. "It must be nearly five years."

"Yes," Rachel said, overwhelmed with the welcome.

"What brings you back to town? And why did we ever let ourselves lose track of each other?"

"I don't have any idea, to the second part of your question. Time and distance can do that, I guess. As to what brings me back, I was here to deliver a workshop on grant writing last week."

Andie's eyebrows shot up. "In Whiskey Creek?"

"No." Rachel laughed. "Jackson Hole. When Josie found out I would be in Wyoming, of course she insisted I stay."

"I don't care why you're here!" Andie declared, giving her another hug. "I'm just so glad to see you."

Warmth swept through her. "I'm glad to see you too," she said quietly, and was surprised to realize it was true.

In the five years since she'd left, she had never dared look back at the good times she'd had there. She maintained a correspondence with Jo only because of the boys. Everything else—even the pleasant memories—had been tainted by Matt's death and the grim circumstances surrounding it. Maybe she'd done herself a grievous wrong. Maybe this visit would finally give her a chance to purge the guilt, to remember all that had been good and right about her marriage.

The bell on the door jingled again, and a rugged, brown-haired man wearing the brown uniform of the Whiskey Creek Sheriff's Department walked in. A teenaged girl followed him, holding the hand of a cherubic little girl with long, dark braids. Andie beamed as she watched them approach.

"Did you find us a good table?" the man asked, and Andie shook her head.

"I found something better! Will, this is my friend, Rachel Carson. She used to live on the Elkhorn with Sam and Josie. Rachel, this is my husband, Will Tanner, and our children, Rosa, Tony, and Emily."

"My, my," Rachel murmured. "You've certainly been busy." When she left, Andie had been a single woman running her own little ranch up the road from the Elkhorn, and also managing a day-care center in town by herself.

Andie laughed. "It's a long story," she said. "If you'll be in town long enough, I would dearly love to get together for lunch and catch up."

"I'm sorry," she said regretfully. "I'm leaving Monday."

A frown flitted across Andie's face, but before she could respond, Sam walked up to say hello to his neighbors. Rachel noticed that he greeted Andie and her family with more cordiality than he'd shown her all day. She knew how he felt about her, so why should this added proof of it send an ache of regret seeping beneath her skin?

"Glad I ran into you," Andie's husband said. "I suppose you heard about the fire up near Daniel. They're calling it the Big Muddy."

Rachel held her breath as the open friendliness in Sam's expression slid away, replaced by wariness.

"Yeah. I heard."

"The boys are keeping a watch to make sure it doesn't come over to our side. That brush up there is so damn dry, though, it'll burn if you just look at it wrong."

"It's been a bad season," Sam said in a clipped tone. The sheriff seemed oblivious to his tension, Rachel thought, to the stiff set of his shoulders, the hard line of his mouth.

"Well, the thing is," Will went on, "with fires along the whole front range, we're spread too thin for my peace of mind and could use every able-bodied man who's ever swung a Pulaski. Any likelihood you'll change your mind and help us out?"

Sam's jaw worked and he frowned. "Nope," he finally growled. "No chance in hell."

THREE

Sam felt as if the entire diner had fallen silent after his overloud pronouncement. The clatter of dishes behind the counter died away, the low buzz of voices stopped. Even the song on the jukebox ended, and he stiffened as he felt the force of several dozen curious eyes on him. He glared back at the few folks who didn't bother to hide their interest behind a veneer of politeness, who watched the conversation eagerly.

"From what I understand, Sam," Will Tanner finally said, "you once were a damn fine man to have around in the middle of a wildfire."

" 'Were' is the key word there, Sheriff. It's been a long time. Too long."

"I gather you had more fire sense than anybody else around, from what folks say. I wouldn't think you'd be able to lose that kind of know-how overnight."

"Five years isn't exactly overnight."

"Well, if you change your mind, call. The crews are

plain worn out and could use any reinforcements who want to step forward."

"Don't plan on it, Will."

To his overwhelming relief, his neighbor decided to drop the topic. The sheriff studied him for several long seconds, then shrugged and turned back to his wife and Rachel. The Tanners walked with them back to their booth. While the women traded phone numbers and the children fidgeted impatiently, Sam was miles away.

For a moment the hubbub of R.J.'s faded and he was once again back on that hillside, the sweat pouring down his back, the exhilaration of the fight against the elements infusing him with an adrenaline high he'd never experienced anywhere else.

He'd been cutting fuel—mostly scrub oak and juniper—with Matt and the rest of his twenty-man crew. They were working on a steep slope, across a drainage from where the fire ravaged the opposite hillside. It had been a scene they'd played out a thousand times, he and Matt, on other mountains, on other fires. Same crap, different day, Matt used to say, with that wide, exultant grin on his face.

The piercing heat, the throb of the chain saw in his hands, his eyes watering, even behind the goggles—all of them were once as familiar to Sam as taking a breath.

Then everything had changed in the space of a heartbeat. The world went crazy as an unexpected wind roared down the canyon, pushing embers across the drainage and sending the flames racing up the bone-dry mountain with hungry, voracious speed.

He'd been crew boss and it had been his responsibility to map out escape routes in case of a blowup. And he had. Dammit, he had. The crew took off to safety, backtracking to the helipad. He radioed for a chopper to come pick them up and turned to make one last check of the fire's progress. That was when he saw Matt on the ground five hundred yards back, his leg twisted underneath him, right in the path of the flames.

Panic flared through him and Sam ran back, knowing he wouldn't make it in time and screaming at Matt to deploy his fire shelter. As the wind-whipped fire rushed at him, the rest of it became a blur. Deploying his own shelter, praying Matt had time to do the same. Suffocating heat as the flames raced over him, choking smoke filling the shelter. Blindness. And then silence—oh, Lord, the silence—as the flames roared off in a different direction.

"Sam?"

Rachel's soft, concerned voice drew him back to the dingy café, and he realized the Tanners had taken their leave. He didn't know how long they'd been gone, how long he'd been sitting there lost in the past.

"Are you all right?"

"Why wouldn't I be?" The words came out gruff, abrupt.

"Well, you shredded your napkin and it looks as if you plan to start in on the place mats next. I just wondered if I needed to start removing the dishes as you go."

The flames in his mind finally receded completely, and he looked at his hands, clenched around the tattered paper. Unable to meet her gaze, he uncurled his fists and let the pieces flutter to his plate. "I'm fine. Just fine."

She looked as if she wanted to say something more, but to his relief she turned back to the boys.

They left not long after. Zach and Noah, exhausted from a day filled with too much going on, nearly nodded off on the car ride home. As it was, he thought for a minute there he was going to have to carry Noah into the house when they returned to the Elkhorn.

"Wait," Rachel said as his sons began to climb the stairs. "You're not getting away that easily. I need good-night hugs from both of you. I need as many as I can get to tide me over when I'm back in California."

Both boys returned to her side and Sam watched, frowning, as they squeezed tightly. Zach hadn't let his father hug him since about the time he was Noah's age. Even Noah, freely affectionate, had complained and quickly pulled away the last time Sam had tried to hug him.

"You have chores in the morning," he reminded them as they finally headed up the log stairs. "You can't get out of it just because we have company."

They both gave exaggerated groans, and Sam rolled his eyes, while Rachel hid a smile.

"No arguments, boys," he said sternly. "You know the rules. Chores first, then play."

"Well, I think I'm going to follow those two and take these old bones to bed," Josie said. She gave Rachel a quick hug, too, then walked to her bedroom, down the hall from the kitchen.

Odd, Sam thought as he watched her go. Jo was usually the last one to bed and the first one up in the morning. All night she'd been quiet and withdrawn. He almost called her back to ask her if she was sick, then he decided it was probably just the excitement of having Rachel there that was tiring her out.

He turned back and found her watching him with those big, serious gray eyes. They were alone, he realized, and felt a moment's consternation. Alone with Rachel Lawrence Carson in a darkened house, with the aroma from the pine of the log walls mingling with some fancy cinnamon-scented candle Jo had bought the last time she went to Jackson.

The intimacy of it rattled him, and he seized on the first excuse he could think of to leave.

"Well, guess I better check on the stock for the night. If you need anything, give a holler. Somebody'll hear you."

"Actually," she began, then faltered.

"Yeah?"

"May I go with you? I—I'd like to speak with you about something."

No, his instincts growled out. How could he say it, though, without sounding stupid, without giving away the shock of awareness that pulsed through him whenever he was around her?

Despite himself, he also had to admit to a certain degree of curiosity. What could she possibly want to talk to him about that could make her so nervous?

He shrugged. "Why not?"

Solemnly, she walked past him, and he tried not to give in to the temptation to sniff her hair, but tantalizing hints of some exotic, sophisticated blend of tropical flowers still reached him. That same scent had

surrounded her when she lived there before, he remembered. It had been one of the first things he'd noticed about her.

His best friend's wife, who smelled like paradise.

Sam swore under his breath and led the way swiftly
to the barn, the gravel crunching under his boots.
When they reached the barn, he checked the feed bins
in the stalls and forked some fresh hay for the horses.

The whole time, he was aware of her watching him,
of the way her features seemed to soften in the dim
light. Still, she didn't give him any clue what she might
want to talk about. It wasn't until they were again out
in the still-warm night air that she even spoke to him
again.

"This is beautiful," she said. "I'd forgotten how the
stars seem so close here. It's like you can rope one and
tug it down to your fingers."

He gazed up, noticing the haze of smoke that clung
to the mountaintops, blowing in from the various fires
in the region.

"What did you want to talk about, Rachel?" he finally asked. "I'm sure you didn't come all the way out
here just to gaze at the stars and walk through cow
manure."

She clasped her fingers together in a nervous ges-
ture. "I wanted to ask you a question. A favor, really."

"What?" he asked warily.

She took a breath, as if preparing herself for a confrontation. "I would like the boys to visit me in Santa
Barbara during the holidays. Maybe for that week between Christmas and New Year's."

He didn't even need to think about it. "No."

"No? Just like that?"

"No. Just like that." He pushed away from the fence and started walking back toward the house.

"But why not?" She walked quickly to keep up with him. "I think they'd enjoy it and I would love to have them stay with me. Of course, I wouldn't want them to be away from you on Christmas, so I thought perhaps they could leave the day after and return before school began again after the holidays. I'll pay for their plane tickets. And Jo's, too, if she wants to come."

Anger flooded through him. He wanted her out of their lives. Couldn't she see that? It wasn't good for the boys to have her flitting in and out like some kind of glamorous, elusive butterfly. They needed constancy, not the unpredictable, distant attention of some woman they barely knew, a woman who showered them with the kinds of things he couldn't afford to give them, like GameBoys and autographed basketballs.

Eventually she'd lose interest in them. He'd be a fool to think she wouldn't remarry someday. What appeal would two hick nephews, related to her by a marriage that was a mostly forgotten memory, possibly have for her then? He refused to stand by and watch her break their hearts that way.

Like his mother had done to him. Sam grimaced. Where the hell had that come from? The situations were not at all the same.

"Sam! Slow down!" she suddenly called out, and he glanced over his shoulder to see her trying to keep pace with his longer stride.

"Won't you even think about it?" she asked when she reached him. "I know they would have a great time staying with me. They can swim in the pool or go to the beach, or we could even drive down to Disneyland. It would be a chance for them to see something beyond Whiskey Creek."

"That's what this is about, isn't it?" The anger flowed back. "Seeing life beyond Whiskey Creek. You hated it here and you can't understand how anybody can be happy at the end of the world."

"That's not true, Sam."

"Well, they are. They're happy, dammit. They have good food and decent clothes and a father who loves them. They don't need you filling their minds with things they'll never have. Things they'll never need."

She stared at him. "You're a snob, Sam Wyatt."

He snorted. "Right. A snob construction worker on a tired-out, old Wyoming ranch."

"You're a snob in reverse. You think because I have money I'm trying to buy their love. It's simply not true. Do you know what else I think?"

"What?" he growled, wondering how he could even notice something like how her eyes flashed when she was angry and how that soft, rosy color stole across her cheeks.

"I think you're afraid," she continued. "You're afraid to let your sons see what's out there, to see anything in the world beyond these mountains for fear they won't come back."

"You know what *I* think? I think you're nuts!"

She shook her head. "You're scared of me, aren't you, Sam? Admit it."

He snorted. "Now I know you're crazy. Why would I possibly be afraid of you?"

"You think I want to take the boys away from you. I don't. I swear I don't. I couldn't, even if I wanted to. They have a wonderful life here, Sam. I just want to be a small part of that, to spend a little time with them so they don't forget me completely. Is that too much to ask?"

Damn right it was too much to ask, he thought. Being part of *their* lives meant being part of *his* life, and he needed that like he needed a third mortgage.

On the other hand, maybe he wasn't being completely fair to the boys. He'd always tried to let them make their own decisions about most things, and he knew they'd jump at the chance to spend time with their beloved aunt Rachel. Especially the chance to see somewhere as foreign and exotic to them as California. And like she said, it was only a little while. Just long enough for the boys to start missing the ranch, to start realizing how good they had it here.

She seemed to sense him wavering, because she pushed her advantage. He froze as she placed a slender hand on his arm, and he could feel the heat of her searing through the summer-weight cotton of his shirt.

"Please, Sam."

He barely heard her, unable to take his gaze away from her hand, delicate and smooth, with elegantly manicured, peach-colored fingernails.

"Just a week, Sam. Seven days," she went on, and he dragged his attention back to her face.

Funny. He'd been with her all night and he hadn't noticed until just that moment how her lipstick was a perfect match to her nail polish. As he watched, she sucked her bottom lip between her teeth, and he nearly groaned aloud, suddenly consumed with an urgent ache, a sweeping, ferocious need to plant his mouth right there, to see if she tasted like peaches, too, ripe and juicy.

She withdrew her hand from his arm and backed away a few steps. "You certainly don't need to give me a final answer today. But please consider it."

She smiled hesitantly, then turned and walked into the house, leaving him standing in the circle of light from the porch.

Angry at her and more angry with himself, Sam stared at the door. He'd nearly kissed her. He'd fought it as fiercely as he could, but he'd been just a breath away from leaning across the space between them and capturing that lush, soft mouth with his own.

Even now, when he realized how truly catastrophic that would have been, a strange regret rolled through him, regret that he hadn't taken the chance when it was offered.

How was he going to make it through the entire day tomorrow—seeing her at breakfast, watching her with the boys—without either giving in to this damn attraction or ordering both her and her fancy car off the ranch?

Simple, he decided. He'd leave. He wanted to drive to Dubois sometime this week, anyway, to check on the subcontractors' progress on the Harrison job. He'd just go a few days earlier than he'd planned. Rachel and the boys could enjoy their time together and he wouldn't have to be around to watch.

To watch and to want.

❖━━━━━━❖

After a restless night, Rachel awoke to sunlight streaming through the dove-gray curtains on the wide window. A quick glance at her travel alarm clock told her it was nearly nine-thirty and she winced. The boys had planned a morning ride with her as soon as their chores were done.

She slipped out of bed. Maybe they would still have time if she hurried. A short time later, dressed in jeans and a T-shirt, she entered the kitchen, expecting to find Jo. The room was empty, but it showed signs of recent sloppy use: Two boxes of cold cereal cluttered the table, along with a pair of bowls, still half filled, and a trail of milk to the gallon container on the counter.

The mess surprised her. Jo usually ran an immaculate kitchen, the plates carefully lined up with the edge of the cupboard, everything within easy reach but everything in its place. Well, maybe some ranch emergency distracted her before she had a chance to clean up, she thought.

She emptied the bowls in the sink, rinsed them out, and loaded them into the dishwasher, then folded down the tops of the cereal boxes. She lifted them to put them away and noticed a slip of paper underneath one of the boxes.

Sam's strong, bold handwriting caught her attention, and she picked up the note.

"Jo," it read. "Going to Dubois. Be back Tuesday. Sam."

Short and succinct. Just like the man's conversation, she thought. No excuses, no explanations. As the significance of the note struck her, she felt relief wash through her. Tuesday. The day after she left. She wouldn't have to deal with him again during her time there, or those fluttery, distracting feelings he evoked in her.

She had just closed the cupboard when the back door rattled and Zach and Noah rushed in. They never walked when they could run, Rachel had discovered.

"Hi, Aunt Rachel!" Noah said exuberantly. "We just finished our chores. Can we go for a ride now?"

"The horses are all saddled and ready," Zach said, then paused, a thoughtful look on his too-serious face. "But maybe you should have breakfast first, if you haven't eaten."

"I'd rather go with you two," she told them. "By the way, where's your grandmother? Is she outside?"

"Don't know." Noah, hopping with excitement, barely paid her any attention. "We thought maybe she slept in like you did."

Rachel felt the first stirrings of unease as she remembered Josie's pale, tired face of the night before. Something must be seriously wrong if Matt's mother wasn't awake with the sun, as had been her habit when Rachel lived there before. Still, she didn't want to worry the boys.

She forced her concern down and managed a small, reassuring smile. "I think I'll check on her, just to see."

They shrugged as Rachel crossed to the door she'd seen Josie enter the night before. She rapped on it and was met with a soft moaning on the other side. The beginnings of alarm rolled through her and she opened the door.

Josie was still in bed, the tangled covers rucked around her waist, and even from the doorway Rachel could see her face was flushed. Sweat soaked the neckline of her no-frills white cotton nightgown, and her springy gray hair was damp and limp.

"Josie? Jo, can you hear me?"

The older woman whimpered again, and Rachel rushed to her side. She placed her hand on Josie's wrinkled brow, then drew it back at the heat there.

"Oh, Jo. You're burning up."

Josie opened her eyes and gazed around the room as if she'd never seen it before. Forehead creased in confusion, she gazed out the window where the sun shone with buttery warmth. "Breakfast. I gotta fix the boys some food," she rasped, and tried to sit up.

"You just rest," Rachel said, easing her head back to the pillow. "The boys are fine. They had cereal and have already taken care of their chores. Now, how long have you been feeling ill?"

"I'm not sick. Just need an aspirin and I'll be fine," Josie said hoarsely. "Sam knows where they are. Have him fetch me one, will ya?"

"Sam's not here. He left a note in the kitchen saying he's gone to Dubois and won't be back until Tuesday. In the meantime, you need a doctor."

"I don't need a doctor. Just an aspirin."

Rachel ignored her. "Who's your doctor, Jo? I'll call him and see if he's willing to make a house call to check on you. If not, I'll drive you into town myself."

"You didn't come out all this way just to babysit an old lady."

"Give me a name," Rachel ordered.

Jo had a fit of coughing, then shook her head. "You're more stubborn than Sam. Call Seth Matthews at the clinic in Whiskey Creek. Maybe he can just give me a prescription or somethin' over the phone."

Rachel nodded and tucked the blankets more securely around her, then walked back out to the kitchen where the boys were waiting for her.

"Zach, Noah," she began. "Grandma Jo's not feeling well. I'm afraid we won't be able to go for that ride after all, at least not this morning. I need to stick around here in case she needs me."

They pouted a bit, but were mature enough to know she didn't have any choice in the matter. They went outside to return the horses to the pasture, and Rachel crossed to the telephone. She found the number of the clinic in big black letters on the phone and soon received the doctor's assurance that he would rush out to check on Josie.

After she hung up the phone, she gazed out the window, at the mountains with their crown of haze and at the two boys in oversize cowboy hats and boots leading the horses, and she felt a smile take over her mouth.

She couldn't possibly leave the next day, not with Sam gone until Tuesday. She would just rearrange her plans and stay an extra day, until he returned. It shouldn't be difficult to trade in her airline ticket for a later one, and she knew her assistant at the foundation was more than capable of filling in during her absence.

She should probably be upset at this upheaval of her plans. Yesterday morning when she arrived—could it only have been yesterday? she wondered in amazement—she never would have imagined she would actually look forward to spending more time in Whiskey Creek.

But she wasn't ready to leave yet. She wanted to spend more time with Zach and Noah. Sam certainly hadn't been encouraging last night when she asked if they could visit her, so she might not see them for a long time unless she made the trip out here again.

Tenderness welled up inside her as she watched the boys jostling each other as they walked back to the house. She never planned to remarry—her first try had been nothing less than disastrous, all the way around— so these boys were as close as she was likely to come to having children of her own. Surely she deserved this extra day with them.

Sam likely wouldn't be pleased to find her still there when he returned from Dubois. The thought should have filled her with apprehension, but Rachel only smiled.

That was his problem. For once in her life, somebody needed her—her, Rachel Anne Lawrence Carson—and she intended to do what she could to help. If that meant staying longer than planned, she was more than willing, especially since it would allow her to spend more time with the boys.

If Sam didn't like it, too bad. He'd just have to deal with it.

FOUR

Home. Sam climbed out of his pickup and inhaled the familiar pine-scented air. He grinned while he surveyed all that he could see: the mountains that reached to the sky, shining a pale gray in the early morning light; the cattle milling quietly; the house he'd built with his own hands.

He loved it all fiercely, in a way he'd never imagined. He never would have guessed back when he was a snot-nosed kid that he would someday find himself so firmly planted in one place. If he'd thought about it at all, he probably would have figured he'd end up like his dad, a vagabond cowboy. Always chasing the next job, always counting on the next prize money just down the road a ways. That was what he'd known, after all, until his dad had died and he'd gone off on his own. Even then, it had been a gypsy, transitory lifestyle, chasing fires from state to state.

Then he'd met Matt, who'd dragged him back to the Elkhorn at the end of one fire season, and Sam had fallen hard. Both for Hannah, Matt's sweet tomboy of a sister with the teasing grin and the flashing eyes, and for the Elkhorn itself.

Now, ten years later, he was just like the poplar windbreak bordering the long, curving gravel drive—rooted deep into the land, into this place that would always be home.

It was peaceful and pristine and ripe with possibilities.

And blessedly Rachel-free.

Sam frowned. If he was so glad to see the back of her, why should the idea of her being gone bother him so much? Make his stomach feel hollow, like he'd skipped a few meals? He grunted and headed into the house. Likely because he *had* skipped a few meals. He just needed to grab a bite and he'd be just fine. Dandy.

The boys were probably still in bed, since the sun hadn't even sneaked above the mountains yet. Maybe he could find time to take them out on the horses later that day. Sort of a payback for running away on them the other day.

When he entered the kitchen, he heard the shower humming in the bathroom next to Josie's room. She must be up and hard at it, he figured, because the kitchen smelled like coffee and the yeasty, intoxicating scent of baking bread. Sam sniffed in appreciation. Jo didn't make bread often, but when she did, it was heavenly—thick-crusted and soft enough to break a cowboy's heart.

Not bread, he realized, grinning. Cinnamon rolls. Now that was an unexpected treat. He pulled one free of the cooling rack and bit into it, tasting sugary, sticky heaven. What an angel.

After snagging another roll and pouring himself a cup of coffee, he slid into his chair at the huge wooden table they'd moved from the old place.

He hadn't realized how tired he was until he sat down. Getting up at three A.M. must have messed with his body clock, he figured. He closed his eyes, just to rest them for a bit. Within a few moments, though, he found himself tangled up in a half-dream about Rachel and all that fiery hair rippling down her back, her gray eyes sultry and aroused as she leaned into him, surrounding him, engulfing him, with the scent of a lush tropical paradise.

"Sam!"

Wrenched back into his senses, he jerked his eyes open. Just like she'd stepped out of his dreams, Rachel stood in the doorway to the bathroom, her hair twisting around her face in wet coils and her face scrubbed clean. She was wearing a faded old T-shirt that dipped dangerously into immodest territory, skimming the tops of her thighs.

He came completely awake with a start, but his hands must have been curled around the coffee mug in sleep, because the next thing he knew, the whole thing slid off the table, coffee splattering across his lap.

Rachel gasped and rushed to him, snatching a dish towel off the oven door handle on her way.

"Oh, dear. Oh, Sam. I'm so sorry I startled you! I was just so surprised to see you since we didn't expect you until later today."

She leaned close to blot at the coffee, and he immediately slid his chair back and stood. "What the hell are you doing?"

"Saving you from a nasty burn. What does it look like?"

He must have been dozing there long enough for the coffee to cool quite a bit, because it was warm but not burning. He felt it seep through the denim of his jeans, leaving clammy wetness behind. The coffee wasn't affecting him nearly as much as this half-naked Rachel.

As her hands fluttered around the waistband of his jeans, Sam felt trapped. With every breath, he inhaled more of her scent, that exotic, intoxicating whisper of paradise.

Completely against his will, his eager, unruly body stirred to life. Damn her, anyway. He rushed to the sink, more to hide the hard proof of his attraction to her than anything else.

"I meant, what are you still doing here? I thought you were leaving yesterday."

She leaned back and watched him, a teasing light in her eyes. "Is that why you're sneaking back so early this morning? You assumed I'd already left? That you were safe?"

"How in blue blazes can I be sneaking when it's my own house?" he growled, angry because she was more right than he cared to admit.

"If it's not sneaking, what is it? What are you doing back when it's not yet six in the morning? You must have left Dubois at four to get here so early."

It was three, not that it's any of your business, he thought, and frowned. "I don't owe you any explanations. You, on the other hand, should be telling me why you're still in my house, using up all my hot water, and, if I'm not mistaken, wearing my damn shirt."

She glanced down. "Oh, is this ratty old thing yours? Sorry. I decided on the spur of the moment this morning to shower down here so I wouldn't wake the boys. I found this in the laundry room and assumed it was a rag."

He glared at her, and Rachel laughed. The sound pealed through the kitchen, rich and full and sexy. That was one of the things that had most attracted him, that sultry laugh of hers, the way it seemed to ripple down his spine.

"I'm sorry. That sounded rude, didn't it?"

"It's my favorite shirt," he muttered.

"It's very comfortable," she assured him. "Speaking of comfort, don't you think you ought to get out of those jeans?"

He nearly groaned. Didn't he just wish! "Don't change the subject, Rachel. Why are you still here?"

All traces of laughter faded from her face and she looked away. The sudden clenching of her fingers on the edge of the T-shirt betrayed her nervousness. "Well, you see, I . . ." Her voice trailed off.

"You what?"

"I stayed to help Josie. She's sick and you weren't here and she and the boys needed me. So I stayed."

"Jo's sick?" He stared at the old woman's closed bedroom door. "What's wrong?"

"She says just a bad cold, but Dr. Matthews at the Whiskey Creek clinic believes it's pneumonia."

Guilt crashed over him, followed quickly by irritation aimed at Rachel. If she had been back in California where she belonged instead of haunting him with her sexy laugh and her smoky eyes and that hair, he would have been there at the ranch instead of gallivanting all over the countryside.

"I shouldn't have left. Dammit."

"It's not your fault. You had no way of knowing she was ill."

"Well, I'm here now. I'm sure you have things to get back to."

Don't let us keep you. He left the words unspoken, but she seemed to flinch as if she sensed them anyway.

"I don't," she said, her voice low. "I freed my schedule at the foundation for at least the next two weeks. That's how long Dr. Matthews says it will take for Jo to completely regain her strength."

Two weeks? Good grief. He couldn't function around Rachel for another two *hours.*

"I can handle it," he said.

"Sam, I'd like to stay. You can't do everything on your own. Jo told me it's your busy time, between the ranch and the log home business."

"I'll just have to shuffle some things around."

"Let me take care of the boys and Jo," she urged. "I want to stay."

"And whatever little Rachel Lawrence wants, she gets, right? Daddy makes sure of that."

For an instant, she seemed to crumple inside herself, and Sam tried not to feel guilty about being so harsh. Then again, he'd seen her do the same thing with Matt, turn all melting and sad when things didn't go her way until Matt would give in to whatever she was after.

When she drew a shaky little breath and turned to face him, he expected to see tears shimmering in her eyes, the tears she'd used so well to twist Matt to her way.

Instead, her eyes blazed with anger and an odd determination. "I want to stay," she repeated. "And you need somebody to help you, although you're too darn stubborn to admit it. I am not leaving, unless you plan to toss me over your shoulder and haul me out of here."

"Is that a dare?" he asked.

She leaned toward him, until their noses were inches apart. "I dare you!"

"I ought to do just that. How are you possibly going to take care of two rambunctious boys? Hell, you don't even know how to boil water!"

"People change. Maybe I've learned how to cook since I was here five years ago."

"Yeah, and maybe my prize bull might decide to start giving milk."

"You think you're so smart, Sam Wyatt, but you don't know a single thing."

"I know you probably have a dozen servants just to blow your nose in Santa Barbara."

Rachel glared. She crossed to the cooling rack where the pastries—minus the two he'd eaten—still exuded their sweet, seductive scent. "Better go grab a milking bucket and a stool, Sam. Just who do you think baked these? Your prize bull?"

"Aunt Rachel?"

At the sound of Zach's voice from the doorway, Rachel whirled. Sam watched as her anger slid away, replaced with soft affection. Despite his better instincts, it tugged at him, the way her brittle edges seemed to shimmer away whenever his sons were around.

"Morning, sport." She tousled Zach's hair. "Did you sleep well?"

"Is everything okay? I thought I heard yellin' down here."

"Your father and I were just having a bit of a disagreement." She gave the boy a conspiratorial wink. "But I think he's just about convinced my way is best. Isn't that right, Sam?"

She glanced at him out of the corner of her eye, as if daring him to contradict her in front of his son. He couldn't, not with Zach watching him with obvious curiosity.

He had to admit, having her stay seemed to be the logical solution. She said she wanted to help. With Jo down, he didn't know what else he'd do, and he knew the boys would be beside themselves with joy to have their precious aunt Rachel around.

He could stand her being there for a couple of weeks, couldn't he? What the hell kind of wuss was he if he couldn't control his body's reaction for two measly weeks?

He dared a look at her, at his raggedy T-shirt she somehow made elegant, at those eyes that brimmed with affection when she glanced at his son. He groaned silently.

Face it, bud. When it comes to Rachel Lawrence, you've got all the self-control of a six-year-old in an ice cream store.

"How would you like a cinnamon roll, sport?" she was asking Zach.

His serious, studious son grinned. "Just one?"

"Why don't you run and get dressed first and I'll save you two. Promise. I'll make sure your dad doesn't eat them."

Zach nodded, gave his father a quick smile, and ran from the kitchen, leaving a stilted silence behind him.

"I'm sorry, Sam," Rachel said quietly. "I know you don't want me here, but I really can't see that you have any choice. I . . . It would mean a great deal to me if you can find it in your heart to let me stay."

How could he possibly refuse when she pleaded with him like she was begging for her dearest wish? "I hope you know what you're getting yourself into," he finally said, and stomped out of the kitchen.

"Where's your father?"

Noah shrugged and slid into one of the ladder-back chairs at the table. "He says he's too busy and, 'sides, he's not hungry. Said he'll eat later. Hey, can I have his dessert? Chocolate cake's my favorite."

Rachel frowned. Not hungry again? That made five meals in a row Sam had been too busy to come up to the house to eat. Lunch and dinner the day before and breakfast and lunch earlier that day. Either Jo's comment about this being his busy time was the understatement of the century or Mr. Sam Wyatt was purposely avoiding her.

She didn't need her degree from Stanford to tell her it was the latter. Piercing needles of hurt slipped beneath her skin before she could harden herself. It shouldn't bother her so much, but seeing herself through his eyes was like looking through a warped mirror, like seeing all her worst faults wrapped into one ugly image. Sam saw only the bad in her, only the spoiled, heedless, frightened girl she'd been five years ago.

But this was getting ridiculous. If he continued this silliness, he'd waste away to skin and bones by the time she returned to California.

Well, she wouldn't let him. With sudden determination, she untied the strings of the big, ruffly pink apron she'd borrowed from Josie. She grabbed a basket from a cupboard and filled a plate with the crispy herbed chicken and potato and fruit salads she'd spent the last two hours preparing.

"Boys, you finish eating. I'm just going to take a little dinner down to your dad. You know what they say. If the mountain won't come to Mohammed . . ."

"Who says? And who's Mojave?"

Zach rolled his eyes at his little brother. "You need your ears cleaned? She said Mohamet, not Mojave."

Rachel laughed and filled a separate plate with a slice of triple chocolate cake, her specialty. "It's a figure of speech, guys. I just meant if your father can't take the time to come up to the house for dinner, I'll take dinner to him."

She quickly prepared a separate tray of the chicken broth she'd had simmering all day, then crossed the kitchen to Josie's door and knocked.

"Yeah?" the older woman answered hoarsely.

Rachel peeked her head in and found Josie using the remote control to flip through the channels on the little television set in her room.

"Don't know why I bother," Jo groused. "Never can find anythin' good on. Nothin' but the news this time of the evenin' and who wants to hear how lousy the world is? Not me, I'll tell you that much. Those folks who watch those all-day news channels have to be crazy, if you ask me. It's enough to make a body sick to her stomach."

Rachel hid a smile. Maybe that was her father's problem. He had two television sets in his office at home and they both constantly buzzed with either CNN or the financial news. Maybe Josie ought to set him straight. She had a quick mental picture of feisty Josie Carson giving her stiff, proper father a talking-to and had to suppress another smile.

"I brought your dinner." She set the tray on the bed. "Now let's see if you can do a better job with it than you did at lunchtime."

A wheezing cough shook Josie's small frame, then she fell back against the pillow.

Rachel adjusted the pillows behind her head with familiarity, as if she'd been caring for Jo for weeks instead of merely days. "That cough sounds a little better. Don't you think?"

Josie shrugged. "Well, least I don't feel like Sam's been draggin' me behind his horse anymore. I'm still weak as a day-old dogie, though."

"It's going to take you a while to regain your

strength. But Doc Matthews thinks you might be able to leave your bed by the end of the week."

"Glory be and hallelujah."

Rachel laughed and gave Josie's hand a squeeze. "Listen, Sam says he's too busy for dinner again, so I thought I would take a plate down to the barn for him. Zach and Noah are still eating. Would you mind if I tell them to come in here with you when they're finished, just for a few minutes?"

"Sure. I'd love the company. I'm gettin' mighty sick of watchin' these bozos on TV."

With Jo and the boys settled, Rachel added a cold beer to the basket that held Sam's dinner and headed outside. The sun was sending long shadows across the ranch as it hovered on the western ridge. It was still hot, though, and a sinister haze lingered in the distance from the fire burning on the other side of the mountains. The air smelled of pine, sweet and tart, but she could still catch a hint of smoke.

She paused for a moment and savored the view. Even with the haze, it was breathtaking: sharp mountain peaks thrusting into a vivid sky, dark pine contrasting with lighter patches of pale green aspen.

How could she have forgotten this beauty? When she'd lived there, those mountains had seemed ominous, an insurmountable barrier between the Elkhorn and the life she'd left behind.

What a strange time that had been. Even though she'd been wondrously happy with Matt, deep in her heart she'd been terrified she had made a terrible mistake in marrying him. She'd looked at her future and seen a lifetime of worrying over every penny, of being left alone while he raced off to the next fire.

Running away with him had seemed so exciting, a romantic way to escape her father's heavy-handed influence. Even with the love they'd shared, though, the harsh reality of Whiskey Creek in winter had been eerie, endless wind, shocking cold, and the overpowering stink of cattle.

She'd been so stupid. She had let her father's anger at her hasty marriage taint her whole view of Whiskey Creek.

The steady rasp of metal on wood pierced her thoughts, and Rachel realized she'd reached the barn. The crew of three men she'd seen working with Sam earlier must have gone home for the day, because he was alone in the work yard. Just like the first day she'd seen him out there, he had stripped his shirt off under the heat of the day.

With her fingers clenched around the handle of the wicker basket, she paused and watched him: the play of muscles in his arms, the sheen of sweat that covered his chest, the concentration twisting those lean, masculine features.

As he'd been the day she arrived, he worked a tool along the bark of a log the size and circumference of a telephone pole. He was so engrossed in the work, he didn't notice her arrival. Finally, when she began to feel like a voyeur, she cleared her throat, and Sam jerked his head around.

The wariness crept back into his blue eyes, and she tightened her hold on the basket. "I brought you some dinner."

He set the tool aside and crossed to a spigot on the side of the barn, then turned it on and splashed his face with water. "I told Noah I wasn't hungry," he said, his face dripping.

"I know you did."

"So what are you doing here?"

"It's not healthy to work in this heat all day without eating."

He lifted an eyebrow. "I didn't realize you'd gone to medical school since you were here before."

"And I didn't realize you had rocks where your brain should be," she retorted.

To her surprise—and to his, as well, she thought—he chuckled. "Well then, you must not know me well enough. Jo tells me that at least once a week."

He reached across the space between them and took the basket from her. "Let's see what we have in here."

He pulled the dishcloth away, and Rachel sucked in air as she waited for his reaction to the food she'd prepared so carefully. When she realized what she was doing, she let out her breath in a rush. She was absolutely pitiful. What did she have to prove to Sam Wyatt, anyway?

For an instant, she was again thrust back five years in time. Sam was right about what he'd said the other day—she hadn't even been able to boil water when she married Matt. A lifetime of having other people take care of all her needs before she even thought of them had left her as helpless as a baby.

After she returned to Santa Barbara five years ago, after she finally realized the world hadn't stopped spinning just because her life had shattered, the first thing she did was enroll in cooking classes.

It was too late to mean anything to Matt, but it was her first step toward becoming her own person, not the girl trying so desperately to please her father or the fragile wife Matt had wrapped up in tissue paper.

"Uh, thanks," Sam mumbled. "It looks good."

"You're welcome." She wrenched her mind from the past and summoned a smile.

He cleared his throat. "I, uh, wanted to tell you. I do appreciate you taking care of the boys and Jo. It's sure made things easier on me."

He sounded as if the words had been pried from him with a crowbar, and Rachel smiled again. "I'm enjoying it. It's nice to be needed, for a change."

Sam didn't know why he said it. Maybe because she looked so sweetly vulnerable sitting there on a stump with her feet tucked under her and her hair hanging loose. Or maybe it was because his body stirred to heavy, sizzling life just looking at her, but he suddenly felt the need to put distance between them and he chose words as his weapons.

"What do you mean you're not needed? You're probably the sole support of all those fancy shops back home. Hell, they'd probably go out of business without Rachel Lawrence and her daddy's money."

She recoiled as if he'd struck her, and her face seemed to freeze into a brittle mask.

"That's right." Her relaxed pose disappeared into stiffness and she clenched her hands into fists in her lap. "And of course there are the valets at all the exclusive restaurants I dine at nightly who put their children through college on the tips I leave behind. And don't forget the people I hire to pretend to be my friends, since a rich bitch like me doesn't have any real ones. Why should I expend the time and energy to cultivate friends when I can buy them so easily?"

"Rachel—"

"No, you're right. Josie had better hurry and regain her health or the whole central California economy is going to collapse without me."

With that, she turned and walked swiftly back to the house, leaving him alone with a basket of delicious-looking food and a stomach too full of guilt to enjoy it.

FIVE

With moonlight pouring in through the kitchen window, Rachel stood and surveyed the contents of the refrigerator.

Warm milk was supposed to be the cure for sleeplessness, wasn't it? She shuddered. The very idea of drinking something warm in the midst of all this heat was repulsive. She'd rather be up all night than have to swallow down warm milk.

She closed her eyes for a moment, savoring the cool blast of air sweeping over her skin from the refrigerator. Noah's gray-striped cat, Nuisance, entwined himself around her bare legs, and Rachel chuckled. "You like that coolness, too, don't you?"

The cat purred in reply. Smiling, Rachel lifted him and closed the refrigerator door with her hip. Nuisance settled into her arms comfortably, nuzzling his head against the thin fabric of her sundress.

A glance at the clock above the refrigerator told her it was past midnight. She had to be up in less than six hours if she wanted to beat the boys awake. At this rate, she'd be dragging all day long.

A slight breeze rustled the leaves of the cottonwood tree jutting into the sky next to the house, and she grimaced in envy. Why couldn't that breeze make it through the screens into the house? The air was stagnant and still inside, underlaid with the sharp scent of smoke.

She wasn't going to sleep. Not as keyed up as she was, not with this tension prowling around inside her skin. She'd been this way all evening, ever since she'd carried that basket of food to Sam and he had thrown his views of her lifestyle in her face like a handful of ashes.

His disdain for her hurt. It seeped like acid into her confidence and ate away at all the contentment she had attained in the last few days, taking care of his sons and Jo.

The really funny thing was, his view of her life in California was about as far from the truth as sable from homespun calico.

True, she lived on her father's sprawling estate—but in a tiny caretaker's house, no bigger than Sam's living room and kitchen put together. And she certainly did spend her days dispensing huge amounts of money, more money than most people would see in years. But the recipients weren't Rodeo Drive clothiers or exclusive jewelers, but the various charities and philanthropic projects endowed by the William J. Lawrence Foundation.

Rachel sighed. It didn't matter. Nothing she could say would convince Sam she wasn't the shallow socialite he viewed her as. And once again, why did she feel she had to prove herself to him?

She crossed to the window and gazed out at the night, absently petting the cat. When she had these periodic bouts of insomnia at home, she would usually take a late-night swim to work out the kinks in her mind and body. Of course, the Elkhorn didn't have a pool and she suspected she'd get a little more than she bargained for if she dived into that pond out back.

It would certainly cool her down, though, she thought. The day the boys had fished, she'd trailed her fingers in the water and it had been cold enough to give her goose bumps.

As icy as she would likely find it, the idea of that water enticed her. If she wasn't brave enough to dive in with the fishes, she could at least dangle her legs off the little pier Sam had built.

Still carrying Nuisance, she opened the screen door quietly so she didn't disturb Josie and walked out into the night. Immediately she felt better, as if the warm breeze had carried her stresses away.

The soft noises of night drifted to her: the hoot of a barn owl, the low whinny of one of the horses, leaves whispering together as they shivered on the breeze.

She had almost reached the pond when she noticed with surprise a half circle of light gleaming on the ground in front of an open doorway into the barn. Her curiosity aroused, she followed the light and peered inside.

Sam sat behind a huge, scarred desk in the tack room, his hands busy with a piece of wood on the table. The light from the single bulb cast odd shadows into the corners of the room and reflected off his dark hair. He whistled softly between his teeth, a slow, sweet tune she couldn't name, but it strummed along her spine like a lover's fingers.

She wasn't aware of moving but she must have squeezed Nuisance, because the cat meowed a protest and leaped from her hands. At the sound, Sam's hand jerked on the piece of wood and he lifted his head.

"Damn," he exclaimed. He frowned, his brow furrowed as he studied the wood in his hand. "Look what you made me do. Took a nick right out of the beak."

"I didn't make you do anything," she retorted. "It's not my fault you're so skittish."

"Skittish." He grunted. "How was I supposed to know you'd be wandering around outside at all hours of the night? I thought everybody was asleep."

"So did I. That's why I came to investigate when I saw the light on over here."

"So why aren't you? Asleep, I mean."

"It's too hot to sleep. Why aren't you?"

"Same thing. I tossed and turned for a while, then figured as long as I was up I might as well try to get some work done."

She crossed the room, the smell of sawdust and leather and Sam thick in the air. "What are you working on?"

"I'm just playin' around," he said, reluctance in every line of his body as she tried to peek over his shoulder, to see what his body was hunched so protectively over. She sucked in her breath when she managed to catch a glimpse of it. He was carving an eagle, perhaps eighteen inches wide, with outstretched wings and a jutting beak. Each tuft of feathers was clearly outlined, some ruffled so she could almost feel the breeze blowing through them, gusting through her own hair. The finely grained wood seemed to shimmer with life, with emotion.

"Sam, it's exquisite," she exclaimed.

"No, it's not. It stinks." He avoided her gaze. "I saw one in the rafters of this show house once in a magazine and thought I'd try to copy it for this place I'm working on in Jackson, but I'm afraid I'm doing a pretty poor job of it."

"No, you're not! It looks so real."

For a moment the harsh planes of his face softened with pleasure at her praise, then that shuttered look returned. "I ought to leave the carving to the experts, I guess. It was a crazy idea, anyway."

"No! You must finish it, Sam, if not for this house you're building, then for your own home. It would look beautiful perched in the Elkhorn family room. I'm so sorry I interrupted you."

"I was just playin' around," he repeated. He sounded so much like his older son, afraid it wasn't masculine to admit he cared about something, that Rachel smiled.

"I think it's wonderful," she repeated. "Josie showed me some pictures of the different houses you've built and I have to say, I'm very impressed. Each one looked like it was built just for its surroundings. Like it was part of the landscape."

Again, he looked pleased. "Most of that's the architect who designs the houses."

"I'm sure a great deal of it is the builder."

He shrugged. "I've been lucky to have good projects."

She perched on the edge of the desk. "I've been wanting to ask you this since I arrived. What is that tool you were using earlier today when I brought your dinner?"

An odd look crossed his face at the mention of dinner, and for a moment she thought he was going to apologize for attacking her as he'd done. Instead, he turned back to the carving.

"It's called a drawknife," he finally said. "We use it to take the bark from the logs since some people like that hand-peeled, sort of mottled look. Others want their logs clean, so for them we buy milled wood from a place up in Montana."

"Can I ask you something else I've been wondering about?"

He glanced up warily. "What?"

"Why log homes? I mean, what led you into the business in the first place?"

He shrugged. "Why not? I needed something after I quit firefighting and I knew how to do two things: work a chain saw and rope a calf. The Elkhorn's not big enough anymore to make ranching more than a semiprofitable hobby. Since I'd done some construction before I married Hannah, building seemed the logical choice."

It was the longest conversation they'd had since she arrived that hadn't ended with one of them snapping at each other. Encouraged by his tame mood, she gathered the courage to ask the other, bigger question that had been troubling her.

"Why did you quit? Firefighting, I mean."

"What?" He dropped the knife and glowered at her.

Well, so much for having a nice, friendly conversation. "You loved it. Why did you quit?"

"What the hell kind of question is that? You know why I quit."

"Matt?" The name lay between them like a wide, deep chasm.

"Yeah. Matt."

When he paused, she thought he would ignore her, leave the topic lying there like a dead snake between them, but then he cleared his throat.

"I, uh, tried to go back. After he . . . after he died, I mean. I couldn't do it. I just kept turning around and expecting him to be right alongside me. But he wasn't. Because of me."

The familiar guilt gnawed at Sam. Abruptly, he realized Rachel had wrapped her arms around herself as if she were cold, although the heat of the night still hung heavy in the air.

"That's funny." Her voice was soft, threaded with emotion. "I thought it was because of me."

He stared at her. "Because of you?"

"Isn't that what you said after the funeral? That I should have been here, waiting for him like a good wife, that you knew the minute he brought me to the Elkhorn that I didn't have staying power."

His hands tightened on the carving. "I said a lot of things after the funeral I regret now."

"Why regret them? They were nothing less than

the truth. I should have been here, instead of waiting for him at that awful motel in Jackson."

He looked away from the raw sorrow in her face.

"I couldn't take it anymore," she went on, her hands twisting together on her lap. "The weeks at a time he'd be gone, the endless fear. It was eating me away inside. So I gave him an ultimatum. The fire or me."

She paused, then continued, so softly he could barely hear. "He chose the fire."

"Rachel—"

She went on, as if she hadn't heard him. "Maybe if I hadn't run away like some spoiled little girl when I didn't get what I wanted, Matt might—might still be here."

He hated thinking about that day and the days that had followed it. The terrible drive out to the ranch to tell Josie, then finding the note Rachel had left for Matt, telling him she couldn't handle things anymore. If he loved her, she'd written, he would come after her. If not, she was going back to her father.

Instead, it had been Sam who followed her to Jackson. He knew damn well she'd been expecting Matt when he knocked on the door. Her face had been ablaze with joy, so bright it had hurt him to look at her.

He hadn't even had to tell her Matt was dead. She just seemed to know as soon as she saw him standing there, and the eagerness in her eyes had faded to a stunned grief that still haunted him.

He'd been so mad at the world after Matt's funeral that when she told him she was leaving, going home where she belonged, he had gone on the offensive.

He took a deep breath now and forced his concentration back to the carving in his hands, to keep from reaching for her.

She must have taken his silence as tacit agreement for what she'd said—that she'd been to blame for Matt's death—because she slid off the desk and began walking toward the door.

"Well, I'm sorry I bothered you. Good night," she said in a brittle voice that somehow moved him more than tears would have.

He stood abruptly, unable to bear her misery a moment longer. "Rachel," he began, then faltered.

She paused, her face still averted from him. "What?"

"Look," he said, walking to her. "Neither one of us will ever know what really happened on that mountain. I thought I did everything I should have to keep the crew safe, but maybe I misjudged something. Maybe I could have moved the helipad a few hundred feet down the ridge, maybe I could have predicted the blowup. But maybe it was just one of those freak things, the way the wind suddenly picked up, the way he twisted his ankle right at the last minute, the way he didn't have time to deploy his fire shelter. I do know it wasn't your fault. You can't spend the rest of your life blaming yourself."

"And you can?"

She had him there. Sam frowned. "The point is, I shouldn't have said what I did that day. I was hurting and you were a convenient target."

Impulsively he reached out and grasped the hand she'd clenched around the doorknob. He squeezed it, amazed by how fragile her bones felt. "If you've been carrying that around all this time, blaming yourself because of what I said, I'm sorry."

"Oh, Sam." She hesitated for a moment, then turned her fingers over and grasped his hand. "Thank you. For trying to make me feel better, anyway. I . . . It means a great deal to me."

Their hands entwined, her gaze met his, and her gray eyes seemed to turn smoky in the dim light of the barn.

Sam held his breath as her exotic, tropical scent tickled his nose. Coconut and pineapples, like some fancy drink in the kind of bars that didn't look kindly on rough-mannered cowboys.

How did she do it? How did this woman—of all the bad-news women on earth—manage to twist him up in knots as easily as a champion bulldogger roped a steer? And how did she do it in the midst of all this charged emotion seething between them?

In the faint light, in the intimate confines of the barn, the pain in her eyes gradually gave way to something more. First stunned awareness, then a frightened vulnerability, and finally a slow, steady flame of desire. She stared at him as if she'd never seen him before, her lips slightly parted and her cheeks flushed.

She didn't even seem to be aware she'd taken a step closer to him, until only inches separated them. Sam knew, though. His damned unruly body thickened, and he jerked his hand away from hers and shoved it into his pocket.

Dammit. He didn't need this, didn't need her looking at him with want in her eyes. He couldn't handle it.

"Sam," she whispered, and he closed his eyes at the startled yearning in her voice.

She had the kind of voice, rich and full, that made him think of silky sheets and naked heat. He could go to her right now, he realized. Could capture her mouth.

He closed his eyes, tasting her in his mind. She would taste like that exotic drink, all sweet and heady and intoxicating. She would respond to him with heat and fire, and he had a quick vision of ripping off that damned sundress, exposing all that glorious skin, and taking her right there in the sawdust that covered the floor of his barn.

"Go to bed, Rachel." The words came out harsh, strangled.

"I—I should do that." She sounded disoriented, and he opened his eyes to find her staring at him with hungry, aching awareness.

"Yeah. You should. Go now."

In the charged silence of the barn, he heard her swallow, heard her feet rustle through the sawdust. And then she was gone.

To Rachel's surprise, Sam showed up at the breakfast table the next morning, the first time he'd shared a meal with her and the boys since he returned from Dubois.

One minute she was flipping pancakes and laughing as Noah regaled her with a story of the mutton-busting competition at the annual Whiskey Creek Founders'

Day junior rodeo. The next she froze as she heard his deep voice greeting the boys.

She whirled around and watched him take a seat at the head of the big pine table. He avoided her gaze, just poured himself a glass of orange juice from the pitcher.

"Mornin'," he said gruffly.

"Good morning." She paused. "Did you sleep well?"

He gave her a long look. "Eventually."

Her skin suddenly felt tight and hot as she remembered those moments in the barn, first the shared pain and then those few awkward seconds of heady awareness. It had been all she'd thought about the rest of the night as she'd tossed and turned amid her tangled sheets.

How could she possibly be so powerfully attracted to Sam? It didn't make sense. He was gruff and stubborn and made no secret of his dislike for her. To him, she was nothing more than a shallow socialite who thought it would be amusing to play house for a while.

So why did she feel all flustered and off balance around him this morning, unsure how to act or what to say? And why did she long to reach a hand out and smooth that little lock of hair dipping into his eyes, to feel that rough skin beneath her fingertips?

She jerked her attention back to breakfast. "How—how many pancakes would you like?"

"Four should do it," he answered, sending her a quizzical look.

"Grandma Jo says Dad can put away pancakes like nobody's business," Noah said proudly. "One time last winter he ate thirteen whole pancakes. All by himself. He just kept eatin' and eatin'. Cool, huh?"

"What an impressive achievement." Effectively distracted, Rachel battled to keep her lips in a straight line. She succeeded until she noticed the tips of Sam's ears turning bright crimson to match the strawberry jam he was spreading on the comparatively modest number of pancakes he'd taken to his plate. Imagine that. Rough and rugged Sam Wyatt could still blush.

"Son, do you have to blab it to the whole world?" he muttered. "Why don't you take out an ad in the newspaper?"

Rachel finally couldn't contain her laughter, and Sam glared at her. "I was hungry, okay?"

"Obviously."

His mouth twitched reluctantly. "You would have been hungry, too, missy, if you'd been up all night birthin' calves."

"I'm sure."

"It was the worst blizzard we'd had in years and neither of the ranch hands could get through the drifts to the ranch, so Josie and I had to deliver eight calves ourselves. Was one he—uh, heck of a night. We lost three of 'em to the cold. By breakfast time, it was a wonder I didn't eat the table."

She expertly flipped the nicely browned pancakes onto a plate, then poured another batch of batter into the pan. "I didn't realize the Elkhorn still had so many cattle. Where are they all?"

"We've only got about a hundred head. Not so many. They're mostly in the grazing allotment up near

Fourth of July Falls. We'll start rounding them up for sale in a few weeks."

"Hey, Dad," Zach said. "You know how we've been wantin' to go up there all summer but you've been too busy to take us?"

"Yeah, Zach. I know." Sam frowned. "I'm afraid I'm not going to have any time for at least the next two weeks."

"What if Rachel takes us? We could go check on the cattle for you and then have a picnic."

"I appreciate the offer to help, son, but I don't think it's such a great idea."

"Why not?"

"That's a steep, twisty trail. It's too dangerous for you boys alone without somebody who knows just what he's doing."

"Rachel knows what she's doin'. She's real good on a horse."

"That may be, but she doesn't know her way around the Elkhorn."

Rachel choked down her instinctive argument. She knew a great deal about the trails on the ranch. She'd had little else to do when Matt was out fighting fires but explore the surrounding terrain. Still, it was Sam's decision, she told herself. He was the boys' father, even if he was a bullheaded man.

Sam finished his pancakes and slid his chair back, then crossed to the door and grabbed his Stetson off the rack, as if the matter were settled.

"Please, Dad. We got our chores done already and everything."

Sam paused by the doorway. "What about

Grandma Jo? Your aunt Rachel should be here in case she needs anything."

As if on cue, Jo poked her head out of her room. Her cheeks looked much pinker, Rachel noted, and she even had a smile on her face. "Who do I hear talkin' about me?"

"Grandma Jo," Noah began, "you don't need Rachel to babysit ya, huh? It's okay if she takes us up to Fourth of July Falls, don'tcha think?"

"Why sure. I'll be just fine. I was gonna read for a while then take another nap."

Rachel hid her smile as Sam gave a disgusted sigh when he realized he'd been outgunned by his sons and their grandmother.

"All right," he said, "as long as you promise to stay with Rachel. Remember, she's a city girl. You boys wouldn't want her wandering off and getting lost, now would you?"

Zach looked alarmed at the idea, but Noah just giggled. "We'll stick to her like flies on manure, Dad. Promise."

Rachel gave an affronted huff and descended on the younger boy. "Just who are you calling manure, young man?" She tickled his ribs and he shrieked with laughter.

"Okay. Okay," he gasped. "Like flies on—on maple syrup."

"Well. That's better."

She glanced at Sam and saw him fighting a smile. For an instant she was transported back to the barn, to those moments when the world seemed to shimmer away, leaving only the two of them, when she'd looked into his blue eyes and seen heat and promise and a tenderness a woman could crawl into and never want to leave.

Those eyes were watching her now, with that same wary approval she'd seen the night before. Finally, Sam cleared his throat. "Well, I've got things to do. Thanks for breakfast, Rachel."

He walked out of the kitchen as if his boots were on fire.

"Hey, boss, you've been hammering the same nail for ten minutes. I'd say it's dead by now."

Sam jerked his thoughts from Rachel and the boys and turned to Lander Fitzpatrick, the burly teenager who helped him out after school and during the summer. "What's that?"

"That nail is in there, man. It's not going anywhere."

Sam frowned when he realized he hadn't moved from this spot in quite a while. He'd been watching the hillside, not paying the slightest bit of attention to what he was doing.

"Maybe we ought to take a break," Lander said. "It's hard to work in all this heat, anyway."

It wasn't the heat wrapping his insides up in knots. The whole afternoon, he hadn't been able to shake a grim sense of foreboding. He knew it was ridiculous. He'd checked and double-checked the gear on all the horses to make sure everything was secure. He'd handed Rachel a detailed map of the area in case they should somehow wander off the trail. And he'd given the boys strict instructions not to stray from her sight.

He trusted his sons. Hell, they were more responsible than most boys their ages. Most boys older than them too. He knew it, but still, the anxiety crawled along the edges of his subconscious, sending him repeatedly out into the pasture near the trailhead to check for them coming down the mountain.

He wasn't going to get any work done the rest of the day until they were safely home, he realized. He might as well go look for them.

After sending his grateful crew home, he quickly rounded up Captain from the field and saddled him. As he spurred the gelding up the hill, he grumbled to himself. They should have been back by now.

What was Rachel thinking to keep them out so late? Didn't she have the sense to realize that the trail, challenging enough in the daylight, could be downright dangerous in the dark? And what was *he* thinking to let them all go in the first place?

A few minutes on horseback improved his mood considerably. Up amid the pines, a welcome breeze cooled his sweat-soaked skin and the air smelled fresh and tart. A few late-summer wildflowers lent bright spots of color along the way and he was accompanied by the chatter of magpies.

He spurred Captain around a hairpin curve on the trail and the trees suddenly thinned out, giving him a clear view down into the valley. Sam reined in the horse and just stared at the panorama spread out before him.

He never tired of seeing this, the Whiskey Creek

valley. The cluster of houses in town and then the ranches spreading out like the spokes on a bicycle wheel, to the very edges of the raw, wild mountains that embraced the valley. In the distance, he could see the tiny shapes of cattle and the sparkling dance of water from irrigation sprinklers in a dozen hay fields prisming the fading sun.

Closer still, he could see the Elkhorn, with its bright red barn, its neat rows of fence, the shimmer of the little pond reflecting the mountains.

A fierce pride swept over him. He had built this. The scruffy son of a wandering cowboy had dug in his heels and worked like the devil to turn a decaying old ranch around.

Technically, the Elkhorn belonged to Jo. She held the deed to the land, although Sam knew eventually it would go to his sons. Both he and Jo recognized, though, that if it hadn't been for Sam and his log home business, she would have had to sell all of it.

Years of bad luck and harsh weather had taken a toll on the ranch, and Jo had sold much of the outlying land years earlier. In the last five years, with the success of the business, Sam had been buying some of it back. Someday, he vowed, the ranch would return to its former glory.

He was a part of the Elkhorn now. For the last ten years, he had worked it and sweated over it and loved it. Even when he was out on a fire, the ranch had always called him back, unlike Matt who couldn't wait to go out on the next blaze.

As if he'd conjured it with his thoughts, a plume of smoke drifted over the mountains from the Big Muddy fire, and Sam grimaced. It would take only a good stiff wind to send that fire down the other side of those mountains into the Whiskey Creek valley.

For an instant, guilt raced through him as quickly as that fire worked its way through dry brush. Maybe he should have given in and helped fight the blaze when Will Tanner asked him. But what could one man accomplish against the wicked fury of a wildfire? Nothing. He'd learned that lesson well. No, he was better off staying right here, where he belonged.

He wrenched his mind from the past as he urged Captain to climb still higher. He had to duck under spreading pine branches in places and guide the horse around the many boulders and fallen trees that covered the dirt path. It took all his concentration. As he'd told Rachel, it could be a dangerous trail if a rider didn't know what he was doing. The worry that had been dogging him like an itch he couldn't quite reach came back in full force, and he spurred the horse on.

The sun had dropped a few more notches behind the hill by the time he rounded the last curve before the falls. Activity on the trail ahead drew his gaze, and he pulled hard on the reins.

Rachel and Zach knelt in the dusty trail beside the supine figure of Noah, and even from twenty feet away he could see the angry, vivid red blood seeping from the ugly gash on the boy's forehead.

SIX

"What have you done to my son?"

The roar boomed through the little clearing, and Rachel jerked up from applying a corner she'd ripped from her shirt to the blood oozing from Noah's cut. Sam glowered down at her, looking like fury personified astride his huge, powerful mount.

"Sam! What—what are you doing up here?"

"I knew something like this was going to happen. Somehow I just knew it." He slid from his horse and strode toward them, anger radiating from him in thick, heavy waves. "Dammit, Rachel. I trusted you. I should have known better."

Her initial relief at having another adult on hand to help comfort the boys dissipated at the disdain in Sam's voice.

"That's not fair," she said quietly.

He muttered an oath. "Life's not fair, sweetheart. If it were, you wouldn't even be here, you'd be back where you belong. In your posh, glitzy life. I trusted you to keep my sons safe."

"Dad, don't be mad at Rachel. It's not her fault."

Noah's weak voice caught Sam's attention, and Sam immediately knelt on the dusty trail, his strong hands moving over the boy. "Where does it hurt, son?"

Noah sniffled, but didn't release the tears Rachel could see brimming in his eyes. "My—my wrist and my head."

"His wrist appears to be sprained." She purposely kept her gaze away from Sam, from the censure she knew would be searing out of those beautiful ice-blue eyes. He was right. He'd trusted her, and she'd failed him.

"As to the cut on his head," she went on, "I believe it looks worse than it really is. Head wounds tend to bleed quite a bit."

"Thank you, Dr. Lawrence," he snarled. After a careful examination he must have concluded her assessment of the situation was correct, because he leaned back on his bootheels and studied the trio. "Who wants to tell me what happened here?"

Rachel cleared her throat. "Well, we were riding back down the trail after stopping at the waterfall for a while and Noah rode on ahead. His horse stumbled on a rock and lost its footing and Noah took a tumble. End of story."

Of course, he picked up on the very thing she had hoped to gloss over. "What was he doing alone?"

"You're right. I should have been paying closer attention. If I had been, I never would have let him out of my sight."

"I told you this is a dangerous trail. You should have been watching them every second. I imagine you weren't thinking about anybody but yourself."

She felt the blood ebb from her face at his harsh words just as Zach opened his mouth to argue with his father. Rachel gave a subtle shake of her head, just enough to draw his attention and stop the boy from speaking. It wasn't soon enough, though, to keep eagle-eyed Sam from noticing.

"Zach? Did you have something else to add?"

"I . . . no," the older boy mumbled, refusing to look at his father.

Sam frowned. "Something else is going on here. What is it?"

Noah sniffled again. "I'm sorry, Dad. Rachel told me and told me not to leave. She hollered at me to slow down, but I was mad at Zach for callin' me a baby and I didn't listen to her."

The tears he'd tried so valiantly to contain for the last ten minutes finally slipped past his guard and rolled down his cheeks, leaving grimy trails in the dust and blood coating his face. "Then Petey stu-stumbled on that big rock, an' I fell and hit my head and hurt my arm."

"Zach, did you call your brother a baby?"

Zach dipped his chin to his chest and stared at the ground. "Yes, sir," he mumbled.

"I've warned you about this, haven't I, about calling each other names? Look what happened because of it. Not only did you hurt his feelings, but your brother could have been seriously injured."

"I know."

Rachel's heart went out to the older boy, and she instinctively tried to deflect Sam's anger away from his sensitive son.

"Sam, I should have been watching more closely. You were absolutely right. I take full responsibility for Noah being hurt. But in the meantime, don't you think we need to be taking him down off the mountainside instead of standing here hurling blame around?"

Sam glared at her but she refused to back down. Finally he nodded. "You're right. The wrist I'm not too worried about, but I'd like Doc Matthews to take a look at that cut. It wouldn't surprise me if it needs stitches."

They followed the twisting trail back down the mountainside in a slow, grim procession: Noah in his father's arms atop Captain, a solemn Zach leading his brother's pony, and Rachel bringing up the rear. Only a thin slice of the sun showed over the mountain by the time they reached the ranch house. Rachel urged her mare abreast of Sam and slid off.

"Let me take Noah while you dismount so you don't jostle him too much," she said.

He studied her a moment, then nodded before gingerly handing the boy down into her waiting arms. Rachel sagged a bit from the warm weight, but quickly recovered. She allowed herself the luxury of squeezing the boy close, of pressing her cheek to his soft blond hair before Sam reached to take him back.

"Aw, I'm okay," Noah said. "I can walk."

"Yeah, you can walk," his father answered. "After Doc Matthews takes a look at that head to make sure it's not a concussion we're looking at."

❖————————————❖

The evening dragged on like rush hour in L.A. as Rachel waited for Sam and Noah to return from the Whiskey Creek clinic. Anxious and edgy, she expended her energy in the kitchen. She scrubbed the floor for the second time that week and smiled as she thought of how horrified her father would be to see his daughter reduced to "menial" labor. William Lawrence would likely find the work degrading, but Rachel couldn't deny she'd found a deep satisfaction in taking care of the domestic side of the ranch for the past week.

She never would have guessed she could feel such pleasure watching the boys try to devour an entire batch of her sugar cookies in one sitting, or seeing Jo eat two bowls of chicken soup after she'd just said she wasn't hungry. And she felt a sharp, piercing joy a hundred times a day—when she hugged the boys before they headed off to bed, when she watched them wade and splash in the pond, when she helped them pound nails in the treehouse they were building down by the pasture.

Dear heavens, what would she do when she returned to Santa Barbara and once again had to be satisfied with the occasional phone call? The thought of it, of slipping back into her empty life, sent an ache curling through her, and she tried to ignore it. She didn't belong here. She was just fooling herself to pretend she did.

Funny, but she didn't feel like she belonged in Santa Barbara either. She hadn't for a long time. She gave a dry, humorless laugh as she wrung out the mop.

A woman without a home, that's what she was. Like a stray dog.

"Any word from Sam?"

Shame at her self-pity rushed through her as she looked up to see Josie standing in the doorway of her room, wrapped in a bathrobe. Rachel shook her head. "None yet. I'm beginning to worry," she admitted.

"Don't fret yourself. Seth Matthews can take his dear sweet time gettin' around to somethin' if he wants."

Rachel smiled at the tartness in her voice. "How are you feeling, Josie? Ready to take over yet?"

As usual, the older woman avoided any question about her health. She pulled out a kitchen chair. "How are you and that son-in-law of mine gettin' along?"

"What do you think, especially after today?" Rachel said glumly. She slid into a chair across from Josie. "Now he not only thinks I'm spoiled and selfish, he also thinks I'm trying to kill off his sons."

Josie snorted. "Naw, he don't. Sam's just protective of his boys, that's all."

"Well, somehow I doubt he'll be nominating me for caregiver of the year."

An odd, pensive look twisted Jo's leathery features, and she studied Rachel with her piercing brown eyes. Rachel was beginning to feel uncomfortable with the other woman's close scrutiny when Jo suddenly spoke.

"Sam's a hard man," she said. "Life hasn't been easy for him."

Rachel sighed. "I know. Becoming a widower at such a young age must have been terrible for him."

"Even before my Hannah died, he had a rough time

of it." Josie paused, as if weighing her words. "What do you know about when he was a boy?"

Rachel tried to picture Sam as anything less than the completely virile, thoroughly male adult he was now and failed.

"Not much," she admitted. "I asked Matt about it once, about where Sam came from. He just shrugged, gave that grin of his, and said, 'Nowhere. And everywhere.'" She frowned in remembered puzzlement.

Josie chuckled. "It didn't much matter to Matt where he came from. Me neither, when it comes to that, but I guess Matt had the right of it. Sam don't talk about it, but Hannah told me a little about when he was smaller'n Noah. His pa was a wanderin' saddle bum and would ride from ranch to ranch as the mood struck him, runnin' from the law or creditors most times, I'd guess. From Texas to North Dakota. California to Kansas. He dragged that boy along with him, whether it was in the middle of the school year or not. Old Chuck Wyatt didn't give a damn, as long as he could follow the next trail."

"Not exactly the most stable environment to bring up a child."

"Nope."

"What about his mother? I can't imagine any woman standing for that kind of lifestyle long."

Josie snorted. "Why do you think his pa couldn't stay in one place for longer than a couple months? Chuck Wyatt used to have his own spread down Albuquerque way. Not a big one, from what Hannah told me, but it was fairly profitable. He had to sell it, though, in the divorce."

"Divorce?"

"When he was three, Sam's mama"—Jo said the word with disdain—"decided she didn't like ranch life no more. She was from back east and wasn't used to hard work. Couldn't stand the smell of manure or good, honest labor, so she lit out. 'Course, she insisted on getting what she considered her due for sticking it out for so long. That is, most of the ranch's assets. She took the money and ran, and neither one of 'em ever heard from her again."

Rachel made a sound of distress at the thought of Sam growing up knowing his mother had abandoned him. No wonder he was so hard, so very protective of his sons. In the turmoil of her own childhood, she'd sometimes felt as if her mother had abandoned her. But having a mother die and having a mother willingly desert you were two entirely different situations. How could a woman make the conscious decision to leave her child behind? Rachel's heart ached at the very idea.

"Yeah, well, I reckon Sam's pa fed him a daily dose of hate for women in general and money-lovin' pampered women in particular."

Pampered women like Rachel Anne Lawrence.

She took a shaky breath as the pieces fell into place. Sam had never been willing to give her a chance. He'd always been quick to condemn her. Granted, he'd had reason five years ago when she had been an immature, scared young wife thrown out of her comfort zone and into an alien world. When she'd hidden her fear behind coldness.

But even after nearly a week of her taking care of his family, her washing his laundry, preparing his meals, and cleaning his house, he still couldn't see her as anything else but that spoiled girl.

"Well, I need to turn in." Josie glanced at her, an odd crafty look in her eyes. "Maybe you ought to head on to bed too. I don't guess you need to wait up for Sam."

"I think I will anyway," Rachel said absently, her mind still filled with the image of a little boy watching his mother walk away.

Rachel sat up through the late news and most of Jay Leno's monologue, although she paid little attention to either. Finally she heard Sam's pickup crunch into the driveway. She hurried into the kitchen in time to see him open the door, Noah in his arms. The boy's blond head, sporting a large white bandage, was nestled against his father's shoulder and his eyes were closed.

It took Sam a few seconds to notice her, but as soon as he did, his long stride faltered. "Rachel," he exclaimed, his voice pitched low so as not to wake his son. "You didn't have to wait up."

"I wanted to. Is everything all right?" She longed to cross the room to them, to take Noah from his father's arms and hold him so tightly she knew he'd squeak in protest.

"It's just like you said. A gash on the head and a sprained wrist. Nothing a few days' rest won't take care of. Let me take him up to bed and I'll come back down and tell you about it."

She waited for him at the foot of the stairs, her mind racing with questions. About Noah, yes, but also about Sam, about the life that had turned him into such a hard man.

Damn Jo, anyway, for telling her about Sam's childhood. She didn't want to feel this compassion, this fragile tenderness. She didn't need it, couldn't handle it. It was so much easier when she viewed him only as Matt's friend, her onetime brother-in-law, the boys' father.

He came down rubbing the back of his neck, weariness stamped into the lines of his face. When he saw her, he dropped his hand, as if afraid to show her any sign of weakness.

"What did the doctor say?" she asked when he reached the bottom step.

He shoved his hands into the back pockets of his jeans. "It took five stitches to close the cut on his head, but Doc Matthews says he'll be fine. Just needs to take it easy for a couple of days and wear that brace on his wrist, but he should be back on that old pony by the middle of the week."

"You were gone so long. I was worried."

"The clinic was swamped. A bunch of wild kids rolled a pickup while they were out four-wheeling. No serious injuries, but it kept Doc Matthews hopping and we had to wait our turn."

"I . . . dinner is waiting for you in the fridge. I thought you might be hungry."

Sam followed her into the kitchen, wondering how she could still look so elegant with her hair scraped back in a ponytail, wearing jeans and an old T-shirt.

It was something in the line of her neck, in the graceful arch of her cheekbones, in the curve of collarbone that showed above the scooped neckline of the T-shirt. She'd always reminded him of an auburn-

haired Audrey Hepburn, somebody who should be surrounded by grace and refinement.

He had to admit, pleasure had burst through him
when he walked into the kitchen and found her waiting
up for him; when he saw that anxious, troubled look in
her gray eyes and realized she was worried about him.
Well, maybe not about him, about his son. Still, it felt
good. It had been a long time since anybody had bothered to make sure he got home safely.

She didn't say anything as she pulled a plate brimming with food out of the fridge: thick roast beef sand-
wiches, her creamy potato salad, and sliced vegetables.
Her hands fluttered over the plate after she set the
table, and she continued to sneak little glances at him.

He cleared his throat. "Somethin' else on your
mind?"

She blinked those long lashes several times, then
looked away. "I—I wanted to tell you again how sorry I
am. About Noah, I mean. I should have been keeping a
better eye on him."

"It's not your fault." The words of apology he'd
rehearsed the whole time he'd been sitting in that
damn clinic clogged in his throat, but he battled
through them. "I shouldn't have lashed out at you like
that. The same thing could have happened with me or
Jo along."

"But neither of you were there. I was. It was my
responsibility to take care of them and I failed."

The guilt in her voice lashed at him like a bitter
January wind. "Rachel . . ." He scrambled for the
words. "I'm no good at expressing how I feel, whether
it's fear or—or love or whatever. I saw Noah lying

there so still and all that blood everywhere and I spoke without thinking. It was easier blaming you and getting all bent out of shape than admitting how scared I was seeing him like that. I was wrong to strike out at you, especially in front of the boys. I'm, uh, sorry I hurt you."

"Oh, Sam." Maybe it was from delayed reaction. Maybe it was from the effort of putting on a brave face all evening for a scared Zach while she battled her own fear that Noah's injuries were more severe than she'd thought. Or maybe it was from the combined stress of the last few days, the tears she wouldn't let herself cry the night before in the barn, and the lingering shock of the feelings Sam had resurrected in her.

Whatever the reason, Rachel felt her emotions crowd the back of her throat and burn behind her eyelids at his heartfelt apology.

She always reacted to stressful situations like this, waiting until the threat was gone, then breaking down. Once, when she'd been about Zach's age, she'd fractured her wrist while riding on the grounds of Lawrence House. She had managed to be brave during the entire lecture from her father about the evils of pushing a horse harder than your own capabilities. She hadn't shed a single tear when the doctor set her wrist or gave her a shot later for the pain.

The moment she'd walked back into her room, though, she'd bawled like a baby and hadn't stopped for hours.

Not here, she prayed silently. *Please don't let me break down here, not in front of Sam.*

She took a shaky breath to try to regain her composure. "Well, I—I suppose I had better try to get some sleep."

She turned to leave just as the first tear slipped past her defenses and trickled down her cheek. She didn't make it more than two steps before more followed.

"Rachel?"

She didn't trust herself to speak, so she remained motionless, her face turned away from him.

"You okay?"

Before she could escape, Sam slid his chair back and crossed the space between them. She felt the heat of his hand on her shoulder and wanted to crawl under the table, away from his scrutiny.

He hissed in a little breath at the tears she wished she could scrub away. "What the hell's the matter now? I told you Noah's gonna be just fine. And I said I was sorry for yelling at you."

"I know. I was just . . . I was so worried. It's nothing. A delayed reaction, that's all."

He studied her for a moment, then muttered an oath. "I can't let you sit there and cry, when it's my son you're crying over. Come here."

She shook her head. "I'm all right."

Despite her protests, he grasped her with his strong callused hands and pulled her close to him. Her cheek was caressed by the soft cotton of his shirt, and his heartbeat sounded strong and steady in her ear. She held herself rigid for as long as she could, until the hard, warm strength of his arms relaxed her like a soothing bath.

At first he patted her awkwardly, as he would a scared horse or one of the boys. Then his movements became more natural and his hand lingered on her shoulder, her hair, the small of her back. Gradually, she felt her body melt into him, felt herself surrender to the healing comfort he offered.

Rachel closed her eyes and inhaled the scent of him, sawdust and pine and that indefinable Sam-smell. How long had it been since she'd been comforted by another person? Her father's idea of showing affection was a rare peck on the cheek in that distracted, formal way of his.

To find such a sweet solace with Sam, of all people, moved her in a deep, primitive way.

As wonderful as it felt, after a few more minutes she forced herself to slide away, compelled by some latent sense of self-preservation. She already was too vulnerable around Sam, especially after her talk with Josie. It would be infinitely worse now that she had discovered he had such gentleness in him.

She hurriedly wet a paper towel in a futile effort to wipe away the traces of her emotion, to still her tumultuous thoughts.

"You must think I'm the biggest baby alive." She couldn't look at him. Not now, with her feelings still so raw, so close to the surface. "I'm sorry I blubbered all over your shirt like that. I must look a mess."

For a moment, only silence greeted her. Then he spoke, his voice a husky caress in the night. "You look beautiful," he said. "As always."

His words seemed to vibrate in the silent kitchen, to soak through her skin. Her gaze flew to his, and Rachel felt as if all the air in the room had been sucked away. She couldn't think, not with him watching her like that, with his eyes ablaze with heat.

"Sam . . ." she began breathlessly.

Before she could finish the thought, he stepped forward and she was in his arms again, lifting her face for his kiss.

SEVEN

Rachel sucked in her breath as his lips slid across hers. She tasted heat and mint and the rough, razor-sharp edge of desire. She held herself stiffly at first, terrified of these feelings brewing inside her, feelings she thought had died forever with Matt. She fought the fierce need to fling her arms around his hard body, to savor his firm, sensual mouth.

What on earth was she thinking? This was Sam, for heaven's sake. Sam who thought she was selfish and irresponsible, Sam who didn't trust her with his sons.

Sam, who had shown her such sweet gentleness.

She tried to draw a breath to pull away, but as her mouth fluttered open, he dipped his tongue inside and all her misgivings flew out the door like dandelion fluff on the wind.

A simmering heat uncoiled inside her, and her arms slid around his shoulders to draw him closer. Need exploded between them, fierce and relentless. With a hungry growl, Sam deepened the kiss, searching, probing, plumbing the depths of her soul.

He pressed her back against the counter, trapping her between the Formica and his own hardness. She gasped as his hard thighs surrounded her, bringing their bodies into intimate contact, as her breasts rubbed against his chest, as her arms of their own volition slid around the corded muscles of his neck.

Liquid fire raced through her, thick and blistering. Through the smoky haze of her desire, some corner of her mind warned her she was crossing hazardous terrain here, but she was helpless to fight it. It felt too good, too right. Too long since she'd felt this alive.

She didn't know how long they kissed. It could have been only a few seconds, but it felt like hours. Slow, endless, languorous hours. She would have stayed there forever, safe and warm in his arms, but gradually the world intruded. The whir of the refrigerator, the creak of logs in the house settling, the ragged sound of their breathing.

She heard one of the barn owls hoot to its mate from the branches of the tree outside the kitchen window, and at the sound, reality crashed back. Rachel jerked her eyes open and shook herself free of the sensual spell he had cast on her, stunned to realize she was a few heartbeats away from losing all sense of herself.

She slipped away from him and backed up several steps, pressing a hand to her throat. His dark hair was mussed—had she done that?—and his too-blue eyes burned with desire. They seemed to glow within his tanned face, mesmerizing her like a rabbit caught in the hard, killing glare of headlights.

She took a shaky breath, searching frantically for her composure and coming up empty.

"What—what did you do that for?" she finally asked, her voice sounding low and husky and disoriented.

"The usual reasons. I wanted to." He paused, scanning her features, her mouth that still felt swollen from his kiss, her skin that tingled, as if she'd just gripped a jolt of pure electricity with both hands.

"And face it, Rachel darlin'," he added softly. "You wanted it too."

She opened her mouth to argue, to deny his words, but the truth pounded into her chest like a fist. He was right. Since last night in the barn—and probably for far longer, if she were completely honest with herself, maybe since the day she arrived—she had been craving his kiss. The taste of him in her mouth, the touch of those hard, rough hands on her skin, the press of his body against hers.

She just hadn't been smart enough to figure that out until now.

"I don't . . ." She fought the urge to cover her suddenly burning face with her hands. Instead, she straightened her spine, lifted her chin, and forced herself to meet his gaze. "That is, it's probably not a smart idea for us to, um, engage in this sort of behavior again."

For several heartbeats, he watched her, his gaze seeming to sizzle right through her. Finally, he nodded. "You're right about that. Truth is, though, I'm afraid I don't feel too smart when I'm around you."

She floundered for an answer, but couldn't come up

with a single thing, so she took the only prudent course. She threw down her dignity and fled the kitchen—and the oh-so-appealing man in it—as if she were running from the very fires of hell.

Though Rachel tried to avoid him for the next few days, Sam certainly didn't make it easy. The first week she'd been at the Elkhorn, he'd gone out of his way to stay as far as possible from her. Now it seemed she couldn't turn around without finding him nearby watching her, his gaze intense and a little frown between his eyebrows, as if he couldn't quite figure out what to do with her.

He treated her cordially enough. In fact, he was more friendly than she remembered him ever being. He teased her nearly as much as he teased the boys, until she would find herself laughing despite her best intentions to remain aloof and distant.

He showed up for every meal on time, his hands and face scrubbed as clean as his sons' and he always offered to help her clean up—offers she declined, for her own peace of mind.

He also began to spend his evenings not down at the barn or in the office going over accounts on the computer, but in the family room where she and the boys played games or watched television after she'd wrangled them into the tub.

He was always busy, carving a piece of wood or studying a set of blueprints or paperwork of some kind, but he was always *there*.

If she let herself, she could almost pretend they

were a real family. Rachel knew it was a dangerous fantasy to weave, knew perfectly well it would only crumble apart like old, fragile paper when it came time for her to leave the mountains. But she couldn't help herself. It was too precious, a rare opportunity to indulge her most secret, tightly held dream. To belong. To be part of a loving family that laughed and teased and loved one another in a way completely foreign to her own upbringing.

Through it all, constant awareness shimmered between her and Sam. She would feel the heat of his gaze on her like a hidden caress and would look up to find him watching her out of fiery blue eyes. The silken threads of tension between them would tighten once again, and she would feel her body kick to life.

Yet he didn't touch her. Not even in the most casual of ways. It was as if he didn't trust himself to simply brush against her shoulder or touch her hand.

By the end of her second week on the Elkhorn, Rachel felt as if her nerves were so tightly strung, they would snap with the slightest provocation.

That provocation came Sunday morning while she made crepes for breakfast. She was busy cracking eggs to mix with the flour and milk, when she heard Sam enter the kitchen. She swore as her hand jerked and shell fragments slid into the bowl.

Sam leaned against the counter. " 'Mornin'," he said in that slow, sexy cowboy drawl he used only when it suited him.

"Hello," she managed to answer. *Brilliant reply there, Rachel*, she thought in disgust.

"You've got flour on your cheek."

"It's, uh, probably powdered sugar. From the crepes."

He chuckled. "Is that right?" He trailed a rough thumb down her cheek, then looked at the white residue clinging to his skin. While Rachel watched, breathless, he lifted his thumb to his mouth and licked it, and she thought her bones would melt into a pile on the kitchen floor.

He grinned. "Powdered sugar. So it is."

She felt her blood surge in anticipation at that sensual light in his eyes, but before she could answer, the boys came charging into the kitchen from their chores, all flyaway hair and untucked T-shirts.

"Hey, Aunt Rach, what's for breakfast?" Noah asked.

With effort, she wrenched her gaze from Sam's and summoned a smile for his sons. She was relieved at the distraction, she told herself. That certainly wasn't disappointment tromping through her.

"Um, crepes. They're kind of like pancakes," she answered.

"Cool," Noah said, his blue eyes, so very much like his father's alight with glee.

Sam grabbed the milk out of the refrigerator and poured it into the glasses she had placed around the table. "Noah, how's that head of yours?"

"Good, Dad. Can I take this dumb bandage off now?"

"Doc Matthews says leave it on a few more days. Feel like you'd be up to taking Petey back up that trail, though, if Rachel and I both went along to make sure you don't overdo it?"

All three of them looked at him in surprise. "Heck yeah," Noah finally said around a mouthful of crepes.

"If the weather's still this nice after church today," Sam went on, "I thought maybe we could take a picnic lunch to the waterfall. I need to check on the stock up there again, anyway, and it seems too nice a day to waste."

Amid the boys' excited high fives, Sam gave her a questioning glance, as if to gauge her reaction to his proposal.

She managed a smile even as she felt her stomach crimp with nerves. Not at the idea of a ride in the mountains. That sounded like a lovely way to spend a Sunday afternoon. It was the thought of going to church that nearly sent her spiraling into a panic.

The week before, in the turmoil of Jo's illness, they hadn't had a chance to go. But Jo was regaining more of her strength every day. For some reason, she still preferred to stay in her room most of the time, but Rachel knew she couldn't use the need to care for the older woman as an excuse to get out of attending services.

Her hands shaking slightly, she spread strawberry jam on a crepe. How could she do it? The last time she walked through those carved oak doors, to bury her husband, she vowed never to pass through them again.

She didn't know if she could face what she knew she would find there. But how could she possibly explain to Sam without sounding like a complete coward?

She couldn't, she knew. He would never understand. She didn't even comprehend it herself. She was a competent, successful businesswoman who every day spent her hours talking to some of the most powerful movers and shakers in the world. By all rights, she should be filled with confidence, with self-assurance.

But somehow, the idea of facing the people of Whiskey Creek made her shake as if she were sitting right in the middle of the San Andreas Fault.

Sam frowned as he maneuvered the good pickup into a parking place at the old white clapboard church in the center of Whiskey Creek. What was wrong with her now?

Rachel looked good enough to eat in a soft, clinging pale blue dress, but she hadn't said two words to him since they'd left the ranch twenty minutes earlier.

She sat scrunched against the door handle, Noah and Zach in all their wriggling glory sandwiched between them, and had let the boys do the talking for the whole ride.

She'd been like this all morning, he realized. Ever since he'd mentioned the picnic. Damned if he could figure her out. Just when he thought he had a handle on who she really was, the confounded woman managed to completely baffle him.

As if some inner light switch had been turned off, Rachel seemed to dim, to close down. Gone was the woman who laughed and teased the boys and who blushed enticingly whenever she looked at him, tantalizing him with curiosity about what she could possibly be thinking to put that rosy hue on her cheeks.

In place of that entrancing, likable woman was the

cold, stiff person he'd known when she was married to Matt.

He wanted the other Rachel back. He grimaced and climbed out of the truck, then walked around the front of the truck to open the passenger-side door. She gave him a startled look as he reached inside and gripped her elbow to help her from the high vehicle, but leaned against him as she slid to the ground.

"Thank you," she said quietly. "I'd forgotten how difficult it can be to climb out of a pickup when you're wearing a dress."

"Yeah," he deadpanned. "I know how much I hate it."

The boys snickered at his lame joke, and even Rachel smiled slightly before her expression once again became closed.

Damned if he could figure her out. Sam sighed and led the way into the church. They were halfway down the aisle to their usual pew before he heard the whispers, like the discontented rustling of a coop full of agitated hens.

"—Matt Carson's wife. That's right, the one who ran out on him."

"How dare she show her face around here?"

"She always did she think she was better than the rest of us."

The last spiteful voice belonged to Karen Peters, whose family owned the grocery store in town and seemed to know everything about everybody.

He could at least understand her antipathy, since she and Matt used to date pretty heavily. In fact, everyone in town had expected the two of them to marry, before Matt went off to California that fall to fight a wildfire and came back with a wife.

In the years since, Karen had become a replica of her mother, a nosy, bitter busybody who wasn't happy unless she had somebody else's troubles to celebrate.

Yeah, Karen he could understand not liking Rachel. But the rest of the women . . . He had no idea the feelings against her ran so deep. What had she done to merit such venom? He searched his memory of her time in town before. She hadn't exactly been friendly, he had to admit. In fact, she'd been kind of bitchy to just about anybody who tried to say a kind word to her.

"—don't know what Sam Wyatt is thinking of to let that woman near his boys after the way she broke Matt's heart."

At the sound of his name and the doubt cast on his parenting abilities, Sam turned and glowered at Karen, who clamped her jaws shut and slid back on the pew. He opened his mouth to give her a blistering lecture about politeness and common decency, when he felt a tight pinch on his forearm. Jerking around he found Rachel glaring at him.

"What are you doing?" she whispered, loud enough for only him to hear.

"How can you just sit there and let them talk about you that way, Rachel, like you're not even here?"

Her fingers fluttered over the pleats in her dress. "Just ignore them. It doesn't matter. I'll be leaving in a few days anyway."

Before he could answer, the pastor stood to begin the services. Rachel held on to her composure through the rest of the meeting, although she felt as if all the stares aimed her way perforated her skin.

Only three or four women had openly disliked her. The rest had tried to be kind, but Karen Peters and her crowd had made no secret of the fact that Rachel would never fit in Whiskey Creek. She'd merely given them more ammunition by refusing to respond to their gibes, for Matt's sake. It also hadn't seemed worth the energy at the time. Now she wondered if she might have alleviated some of the tension by standing up to them, or at least by trying to make some effort to be nice to the women instead of completely ignoring them.

After the meeting, she hoped Sam would hurry out of the church so she could leave the uncomfortable atmosphere. Instead, the fates conspired against her. First, the young pastor, new since her time there, wanted to meet the "lovely young woman our Sam brought along." Rachel forced herself to smile during the introductions and the polite talk that came after.

Just as they made their good-byes and began walking out to the parking lot, she heard her name called and turned to find Andie Tanner hurrying toward her.

Her stiff smile melted into a genuine one at the sight of her friend.

"I thought you'd left!" Andie exclaimed. "Why on earth haven't you called me?"

She winced. "I haven't had much of a chance. Josie's been sick and I offered to stay and help Sam with the boys."

"Jo's sick? Oh no! If I'd known, I could have come out to help. What's wrong?"

"Dr. Matthews says pneumonia. She seems to be feeling much better now. I'm sure I'll be leaving in a few days."

She didn't miss the way Sam stiffened or the frown that added lines to his forehead. Before she could analyze his reaction, Andie's husband joined their group.

He shook Sam's hand. "Sam. Guess you've heard by now they had to take two hundred of the men they had fighting the Big Muddy fire down to Kemmerer to fight the blaze they have down there."

"I heard."

"They're way too shorthanded now. I know they sure could use you."

"Don't push him, Will," Andie said, a chiding hand on her husband's arm.

"I'm sure the crew they've got up there can do just fine without me," Sam said.

The sheriff looked as if he wanted to argue, but a pinch from his wife silenced him. After a few more minutes of conversation—with Rachel promising she'd call Andie before she left—Sam ushered them away. Rachel didn't know if that frown he wore was because of Will's comments or because she was leaving. She wasn't sure she wanted to know.

Later, as she packed food for their impromptu picnic, she couldn't shake the ache of depression that had settled on her shoulders. After her reception in church, the thought of saying good-bye to Whiskey Creek ought to fill her with nothing but relief.

Why, then, did she have this insistent feeling that she would be leaving behind the most important part of her life when she returned to California?

She would miss the boys terribly, of course. She'd loved them before, but since she'd had a chance to spend uninterrupted time with them, that love had swelled, deepened. She would also miss Jo and her acerbic wit, her no-nonsense, practical attitude toward life.

And she would miss Sam. The thought shocked her, but it resounded with truth.

She would miss these wild feelings he sent surging through her with just a look. She would miss their banter, their shared smiles over the boys' antics, even the way he teased her until she blushed.

The screen door in the kitchen banged suddenly, and Zach ran in. "Dad sent me in to see if I can carry anything for you."

Rachel wrenched her mind from thoughts of her inevitable departure and smiled at the boy. "You take the sodas and I'll bring the rest."

She wouldn't worry about it, she told herself as she carried the basket of food outside, where Noah held her horse's reins. She would savor this time with them, wrap it up carefully and store it away in her mind to take out and relive when she returned to reality.

She had plenty of memories to store up that day, Rachel thought later as she returned the uneaten food to the basket after their picnic. The slow, easy pace of the ride up the mountain trail, with Sam pointing out signs of wildlife and talking about the history of Whiskey Creek as they rode. The breathtaking beauty of the scenery. The sheer pleasure of laughing with Sam as the boys tried to eat their pieces of cake in two quick bites.

"Ease up, Rachel. Relax for a minute."

She glanced up to find him watching her now, an unreadable look in his hooded eyes. He was sitting on the old blanket they had spread under the wide branches of a towering spruce tree, leaning against the trunk and looking completely relaxed, perhaps the first time she'd ever seen him that way.

"I'm almost finished here," she replied, trying not to gawk at him like a lovestruck teenager.

With that short-sleeved red cotton shirt stretched over his broad chest and those worn jeans and low-heeled cowboy boots, Sam looked rugged and male. Toss in that slightly wicked grin and those heavenly blue eyes, and the man was darn near irresistible.

He crossed those boots at the ankle, eased back against the tree, and closed his eyes. "The boys are right. I haven't made nearly enough time lately to come up here."

"It's a beautiful spot." Rachel forced her attention away from Sam and gazed out at the scene, at the pines that sent their tart scent flowing through the clearing, at the waterfall that cascaded twenty feet down the rocky, brush-covered hillside, at the boys fishing several hundred yards away in the clear mountain stream.

She was enjoying the view so much she was completely unprepared for his frontal attack.

"So when are you going to tell me what that was all about today in church?"

She drew a quick breath and turned back to him. "It doesn't matter, Sam. Drop it. Please?"

"It matters to me."

"I really would rather not talk about it, if it's all the same to you."

"Too bad. Tell me anyway."

She sighed. The man could be as tenacious as a bulldog when he had his mind set on something. She knew he wouldn't let up until he'd gnawed the topic to death.

After a moment she spoke, picking her words carefully. "It's taken me a long time to realize I was to blame for most of it. As you reap, so shall you sow, or so my minister back home was fond of saying."

"To blame for what?"

She fiddled with the handle of the picnic basket. "You have to understand, Sam. When I lived here before, I didn't know who I was. I'd always been only Rachel Lawrence, William Lawrence's quiet, obedient daughter. Suddenly in Whiskey Creek I became Rachel Carson, the spoiled rich girl Matt Carson was foolish enough to drag out here. Inside I was just me. Scared and young and afraid I had just made the biggest mistake of my life by marrying Matt."

Sam gave her a startled look, questions flying through him. "I thought you loved him."

"I did. A part of me always will." She stared down at her hands. "When we were together I had no doubts I'd been right to marry him. But when he started to go out on fires, when he would take all that laughter and leave me alone, the fears would be overwhelming."

For the first time, he began to see how it must have been for her, a twenty-year-old bride who'd been pampered all her life, thrown headlong into the rough-

and-tumble world of a floundering ranch. It would have been like being thrust into a new country where you didn't speak the language, didn't know the natives, and didn't have the faintest idea how to go about fitting in.

And she'd had the antipathy of at least some of the women in Whiskey Creek to contend with—not to mention his own barely concealed disdain. Regret pulled at him. He could have been a hell of a lot more understanding, especially after Matt's death. Instead, he'd lashed out from his own pain and guilt.

"What about since you left? How have you been?" He frowned, suddenly struck by how self-absorbed he'd been since she came. "Do you know, you've been here for two weeks and I've never even asked you about your life?"

She gave him a sidelong, teasing glance that took him completely by surprise. "Yes, you did. Except you asked me about the life you think I have. I'm afraid the reality is a far cry from all the glitz you imagine."

"So tell me the reality."

"I love my work at the foundation," she said, her eyes suddenly burning with zeal. "When I started, there was nothing. A few little projects my father gave a halfhearted effort to and that's about it. It's been so rewarding building the foundation from next to nothing to the powerful force it's become. Do you know we're one of the top twenty charitable trusts in the nation?"

"Guess it didn't make the papers around here. Sorry."

"Well, we are. We fund everything from a safe-house for battered women to several condominiums at Disneyland for children with terminal illnesses and their families. Last month, we set up an organization to use music therapy for Alzheimer's patients. They're making incredible progress, touching on memories that have been buried for years in these people."

She went on, bubbling with enthusiasm, for several more minutes while Sam sat back and fought a grin. He adored this side of her, he realized. This animated, vibrant woman filled with a need to make the world a better place.

She paused. "I'm sorry. I'm afraid I get a little carried away."

"I like to hear about it. I only wish I'd asked you earlier," he said truthfully.

"If I'd known that, I would have talked your ear off long before now." She smiled. "Some days I have so much bursting inside me I have to go up to Lawrence House and corner one of the servants. They all run when they see me coming now."

He stared. "You don't live with your father."

"Heavens no. Well, not technically, anyway. I live in a little cottage on the estate, a notion that still horrifies him. 'You're a Lawrence, girl.'" She mocked a man's serious tone. "'It's time you realized that and stopped hiding from your responsibilities.'"

"Your dad sounds like a real prince."

Rachel smiled, without humor. "If he could buy a princedom, believe me, he'd certainly try."

The excitement that had animated her features when she talked about her work had faded. "Actually, Father's not that bad. In my heart, I know he only wants what's best for me. The trouble is, we have vastly different opinions about what exactly that might be."

Sam fiddled with a cone he'd found under the tree. "Why did you go back there? I've always wondered how you could do it. He basically cut you off when you married Matt, didn't he?"

"How could I swallow my pride and go crawling back?" she said, a trace of bitterness in her voice. "Must be the money, right?"

"A week ago, I would have said that. Now I don't think so."

She looked away from him, at the horses nibbling the sweet high-meadow grass, at a hawk circling overhead in search of food of his own. When she turned back, her expression was solemn.

"I didn't have anywhere else to go," she said simply.

"You could have stayed here."

"No, I couldn't. I had nothing left here, not after Matt died. Anyway, it hasn't been so bad. Not after the first round of 'I-told-you-so's.' We basically stay out of each other's way."

"Are you happy?" He didn't know why he was compelled to ask the question. Maybe it was the lingering sadness in her gaze or the way she sat with her hands folded tightly in her lap. Or maybe because he needed to know she'd found some peace.

"I thought I was," she said. "If not happy, at least content."

"Thought? Past tense?"

She paused for a long time, and when she spoke, her voice was low, like a distant wind. "I didn't realize how alone I've been until I came here. Until I saw the boys and Jo and you again."

A low, throbbing ache spread out in steady waves from the center of his chest throughout his body. "Rachel—" he began.

"Heavens, I sound pathetic, don't I?" She gave a hollow-sounding laugh. "I'm sorry, Sam. I didn't mean to dump all this on you."

He wanted to pull her onto his lap and kiss away the clouds in her eyes, to bring a genuine smile to that mouth. Before he had a chance to think it through, he reached for her hands and tugged her toward him.

She landed against his chest with a startled exclamation that died when their gazes met. She hitched in a little breath just as his mouth touched hers.

EIGHT

He meant only to offer comfort, but at the touch of her mouth, warm and yielding under his, any altruistic motives flew completely out of his head. She tasted like peaches from the pie they'd had earlier, sweet and delicious. He rubbed his mouth over hers, savoring the flavor, and she made a gasping sound of arousal that seemed to seep into his bones.

Her hands fluttered over his shoulders as if she couldn't decide what to do with them, then he smiled against her mouth when her arms slid around his neck. She twisted her fingers into the hair at his nape, stroking it, stroking him.

He'd dreamed of nothing but this since the other night in the kitchen, when she'd melted in his arms like snow in July. He'd taken more dips in that damn pond out back than he cared to remember, trying to keep from going to her.

The icy pond would do nothing to ease this need in

him, he realized. His body was thick with it, especially with her pressed against him.

Groaning, he tightened his arms around her and deepened the kiss, feeling the erotic glide of her tongue against his. He was a half second from sliding his hand along the smooth skin under her shirt when shouts of laughter intruded.

"Sam. Stop. You have to stop." Her voice sounded breathy, sweetly aroused.

He thought about arguing with her, but it didn't seem worth the effort with her all soft and giving in his arms. He gave in to the impulse and tugged her shirt free of her waistband, then dipped his hand along the heated skin of her back. She shivered, her head tilted back, and he dragged his mouth away from hers to trail kisses down her neck.

He had his fingers on the buttons of her shirt when the sound of the boys' cheerful chatter as they walked up the trail finally penetrated his consciousness.

Sam froze until the waves of desire pounding through his body began to slow. Taking a shaky breath, he dropped his arms to his sides, and Rachel quickly scrambled off his lap and to the far side of the blanket.

He groaned, this time with frustration, wishing he could just pound his head against the spruce tree. What was he thinking, to kiss her until they were both sense-less with need while his boys played and fished only a few hundred yards away?

Not that he regretted kissing her again. The feel of her in his arms had been all he could think about the last week. But he sure as hell could have picked a better place.

He watched her tuck in her blouse with hands that trembled like the aspen leaves dancing in the woods, and a primitive satisfaction spilled through him. It was nice to know she'd been as affected by their kiss as he.

He sighed and twisted a strand of her auburn hair around his finger, hair that caught the hot afternoon sun.

"What are we going to do about this, Rachel m'dear?" he murmured.

"About what?"

"About the heat that simmers between us whenever we touch?"

She tried to slip free, but he tightened his hold on the silky threads of her hair. She glared at him. "Why do we have to do something about it? Can't we just go on like before? Pretend this never happened?"

He snorted. "If you can pretend there's not something going on here, something more potent than home-brewed whiskey, you've got a hell of a lot better imagination than I do."

Before she could answer, the boys rounded the curve of the trail into their view, and he slipped the errant strand of hair behind her ear. She closed her eyes and shivered slightly at his touch. At that delicate little motion, Sam wanted to forget the ranch and the boys both and drag her down onto the blanket.

The wind picked up as they prepared to leave the mountain. It should have been refreshing, but it just seemed to swirl the stagnant heat along with it.

Rachel spent the rest of the afternoon in an obvious attempt to avoid his touch, while Sam worked fiercely to rid his mind of the image of her in his arms, tousled and wild. His complete lack of success made for one mighty uncomfortable ride down the mountainside.

He felt more charged with energy than he remembered in a long time, but he wasn't stupid enough not to recognize his own foolishness. He wanted Rachel with an ache that bordered on pain. He knew it, but he didn't understand it.

If he had to have a woman in his life, he should have picked somebody undemanding, uncomplicated, straightforward. A rancher's daughter, maybe. Somebody who belonged there and wouldn't be packing her soft hair and her softer gray eyes into her fancy convertible and speeding out of his life as soon as she could arrange it.

Maybe that was why he was so attracted to her, he thought, with sudden, unpleasant insight. She was unattainable to him, and maybe that made her safe prey. Off-limits. Somebody who wouldn't expect anything of him, especially not the love he'd locked away in a hidden corner of his soul after Hannah died.

Rachel Lawrence and her silver-spoon lifestyle were as distant to him as the moon. Lord knows, she wouldn't be happy with a Wyoming cowboy again. She'd traveled that trail before and had emerged on the other side bloodied and damn near broken.

He was frowning, still trying to puzzle it out, as they rode up to the house. To his surprise, Jo stood on the porch dressed in jeans and a work shirt, her usual attire. He glanced at Rachel to see if she realized the significance of Jo being up and about, if she knew her time there was drawing to a close, but she was looking at something off in the distance and he couldn't see beyond her profile.

He was just about to tease Jo about waiting until they left before climbing right out of bed, when he noticed the solemn set of her expression, the worry creasing her brow. "What is it, Jo?" he asked instantly.

She walked down the porch steps to Captain's head. "I just heard on the radio. That wind is taking up embers from the Big Muddy fire and carrying them all over the place. The fire's moved down the hill now, and so far it's burned out the McClosky place—house, barn, and all—and is headin' for Cord Staples's spread."

He muttered an oath and slid from Captain. Rachel and the boys, their laughter fading into somber concern, did the same.

Dammit. He'd been so busy watching Rachel all the way down the mountain that he hadn't bothered to look out across the valley.

"Is the Staples place close to here?" she asked.

"No, it's on the other side of the valley. A good ten miles away. Sounds like the fire's on the move, though. Dammit, and they just sent two hundred guys off to another fire."

"Do you think there's any danger?"

"Not to us, but there are six other ranchers not far from Staples hanging by a thread anyway. Something like this is going to ruin them."

"You gonna go help?"

He glanced at Jo. "I don't have much of a choice, do I?"

"You're not going to go fight that fire, surely."

He turned to Rachel. The fear in her voice was unmistakable. "No, but I can do what I can to help round up livestock on the ranches in the fire's path. I imagine they're going to truck as many as they can to safer ground."

It took him nearly half an hour to hitch the horse trailer to his pickup and load Captain. Sam was throwing his lasso and leather gloves into the cab when he heard footsteps behind him. He turned to find Rachel watching him, her eyes immense and dewy in her pale face.

"Be careful, Sam. Don't do anything foolish. Those boys of yours need you."

He smiled at her. "I'm just goin' on roundup, Rachel. I won't even get near the fire."

She place a slim hand on his arm. "Just be careful. Please?"

For an instant, he wondered what it would be like to have her waiting for him. Not just here, in his house, but in his heart. To be able to catch her in his arms at the end of the day and not let go until morning. Their gazes locked, and he felt that connection with her again, like a weird electrical charge in his chest.

He covered her hand with his own. Her skin felt cold and he squeezed her fingers, wishing he had the right to want her waiting there for him and angry at himself for craving what he couldn't have.

"I'll be careful, Rachel. Promise."

Before he could do something foolish like grab her and kiss that worry out of her eyes, he climbed into the truck and drove away, leaving her watching after him.

"Gal, you're tirin' me out. And you're gonna wear this fancy new carpet to bare threads if you don't quit that blasted pacin'."

Rachel let the curtain drop and glanced at the sofa where Jo sat with a tabloid newspaper in her lap. Canned laughter squawked from the television set she'd been pretending to watch for the last hour, since the boys reluctantly went to bed.

"It's past ten," she said. "Shouldn't he be home by now? They certainly can't round up cattle in the dark, can they?"

Jo shrugged. "With that full moon, it's almost as bright as day out there. Who knows when they'll wind it up."

She wasn't worried, Rachel thought. Sam could take care of himself. It was just so much like before, trying to sit at home like a dutiful wife while Matt eagerly traipsed off to whatever hot spot currently had his name on it.

She had hated it then and she hated it even more now.

Not that she felt anything for Sam like she had for Matt, she reminded herself sternly. Matt had been everything to her. He had been funny and warm and so full of life.

Sam was just . . . Sam. He was stubborn and abrasive and aggravating. Well, not always. For an instant, she was back in his arms as she'd been that afternoon, his mouth firm and urgent on hers as he drew response after response from her.

Rachel shivered in remembered pleasure and folded her arms tightly across her waist. So what if he had the most incredible eyes she'd ever seen and made her feel as if she'd been encased in a protective block of ice for the last five years, protection that now seemed to be melting away under the hot sun? It was purely physical. It had to be.

She was just concerned for the boys, that's all. She wouldn't want anything to happen to their father after they'd spent most of their lives motherless.

Right. And the Wind River Range might crumble away into a little pile of dirt tomorrow.

That was why Sam was the last thing she thought of before she fell asleep each night and the first person to enter her mind upon waking each day. Why she found herself increasingly eager to share something the boys did with him, why she blushed and stammered and otherwise completely lost her composure whenever he smiled at her.

She wasn't just physically attracted to him, Rachel thought. Something about his solid strength, about his hidden gentleness, tugged at her, seeped into her heart.

"Well, I think I'm gonna head on in to bed. I'll just leave you to your pacin'."

She glanced up to find Jo standing, her skinny arms above her head in a stretch.

"How are you feeling?" Rachel asked. "I'm sorry I haven't asked before now. You seem much better than you were even yesterday."

The older woman's gaze sharpened. "You that eager to get out of here?"

Rachel bit her lip. Was she? On the one hand, she

wanted to stay forever in this make-believe family. On the other, she knew she needed to return to California, to the life she knew—and to escape these wild feelings Sam aroused in her. They made her too vulnerable, her emotions too exposed.

"If you're back on your feet, there's really no reason for me to stay around," she finally said.

"You probably got things you need to get back to. I understand. Don't think I don't appreciate what you've done here. And Sam does too. Even if he don't say nothin' about it."

Jo crossed the room to the window where Rachel stood. She gave her a quick hug, then stepped back. "I know you hated it here when you were married to my boy. I'd a been crazy not to see that. You still hate it?"

Rachel pulled the green-checked curtain back and looked out at the night, at the rough mountains that gleamed in the moonlight, at the horses in the pasture, at the pond with its ring of boulders.

"You know, I don't," she said, surprised. "I used to feel so claustrophophic here. Trapped by the mountains. It seems different now."

"The mountains never change, child. Only people change."

"Have I?"

Josie paused, as if debating her words, then nodded. "I accepted you back then 'cause my boy brought you here and 'cause it was clear to anybody with a brain in his head you loved him. But to be truthful, I never liked you much. You just didn't give anybody a chance to like you. Nobody but Matt, I guess."

Completely unprepared for the words, Rachel

stared at Jo while hurt swelled inside her. Some sign of it must have shown on her face, because Jo smiled apologetically and squeezed her hand.

"Like I said, I didn't like you much. Then. But you're different now. Softer, somehow. I like you plenty. You're family, whether you want to be or not, and you'll always be welcome at the Elkhorn."

"Thanks, Josie." Rachel managed a smile, her emotions still whirling.

"And, to tell you the truth, I'll miss you when you go. It's been a downright joy havin' another woman around the place again."

She cleared her throat, withdrawing her hand and slipping it into the pocket of her robe. "Now I'm goin' off to bed before I start blubberin'."

When Jo left the room, Rachel again lifted the curtain. She ought to go to her room, as well. She had no reason to wait up for Sam like a concerned wife. But she knew she'd never be able to sleep, not with the worry that had settled on her shoulders like a heavy, strangling cloak.

The stars winked invitingly and the branches of the pine tree near the house scratched against the window in the breeze. That breeze beckoned her, and she opened the back porch door. With no destination in mind, she began to walk. If she had to pace, she ought to at least do it out here in the fresh air, she thought with a rueful smile, even if the air did carry the sharpness of burning timber.

She followed the pasture fence around to the huge old barn and slipped inside. The familiar smells of wood shavings and livestock surrounded her in a pungent but somehow comforting welcome. She paused a moment to savor the quiet rustle of the few animals Sam kept inside the barn, then flipped on the light.

The tack room where she'd found him the other night—where she'd first felt this heady closeness—beckoned to her.

In that room the ripeness of animals faded, replaced by leather from the saddles, harnesses, and bridles lining the wall. A long, plump couch took up most of one wall. During calving season, she remembered, Sam or Matt would take turns sleeping on that couch.

Matt never enjoyed ranch work like Sam had, she mused. He'd done it during the winter when the fire season ended, but he'd always been restless, eager for action.

She was discovering they were very different, Sam and her late husband. Sam was more serious than Matt had been, but there was a streak of teasing playfulness in him that completely charmed her. Matt had been impulsive, always ready to try something new. Sam, she was learning, liked to take his time about things, liked to make certain something would work before he put his energy behind it.

And then there was this desire for him that seethed and tugged beneath her skin. She shivered at the memory of his hands, of his mouth, of his hair beneath her fingertips that afternoon. If the boys hadn't been there, she knew she wouldn't have been able to stop him. Wouldn't have wanted to stop him, even if she could.

Suddenly insatiably curious about him, Rachel crossed to the makeshift desk in the corner. What kinds of clues would Sam have left behind to help her unravel the mystery of his psyche?

The desk was neat, covered only with a set of blueprints, a telephone, and what looked like a dozen gnawed pencils in a soup can adorned with elbow macaroni spray-painted gold. One of the boys must have made it for him, she thought, and smiled softly.

He was a good father, that much she could say without question. His sons and their happiness came first in his life, she had no doubt of that in her mind.

For an instant, a tiny, niggling guilt at her nosiness skittered along her nerves, but she pushed it away and slid into the leather desk chair with a long, jagged rip along the front. From this vantage point, she noticed the blueprints bulged oddly in the midde and, suppressing her insistent conscience, she lifted the papers to find the carving tools he'd been using the other night along with a collection of tiny wooden figures.

A nativity set! Sam was carving a nativity set. She could see the serene Mary and a little wooden baby in a manger. It was all there—the wise men, a camel, even some tiny sheep that didn't look quite finished.

She sighed with pleasure. They were beautifully realistic, right down to the fingers the shepherd used to hold a staff. How had Sam possibly had the patience to work such delicate magic?

She raised each figure for a closer look, then paused when she reached a small angel with dainty, lifelike features. Frowning in puzzlement, Rachel studied it closer. She ran her thumb over the face of the angel. Something didn't seem right about it, but she couldn't quite determine what. It was exquisite work, ethereal in its loveliness. It just didn't look very . . . angelic.

She was still trying to analyze why not when she heard a truck's engine outside. Jumping guiltily, she quickly returned the little angel to the pile of wooden figures and hurried out of the barn just as Sam opened the door of the pickup.

He looked tired, she thought. Dust covered him, from his Stetson to his boots. The laugh lines bracketing his mouth looked deeper than they had earlier, and still not noticing her, he rotated his neck as if his shoulders could hardly support the weight of his head. An unaccustomed tenderness washed through her, and she fought a powerful urge to cross the distance between them and draw that dusty dark head to her own shoulder to ease his burden.

She shoved her hands in the pockets of her shorts as if to keep from reaching for him. He must have noticed her movement, because he turned and shock rushed across his features at the sight of her.

"Rachel! What are you doing down here?"

"Waiting for you," she admitted. "I was too restless in the house, so I decided to take a walk and found myself here. How was it?"

"We were cutting it close, but I think we got most of the Triple S stock, except for about twenty-five head we just couldn't find."

"Will they be all right? They're probably terrified."

He laughed, and it sounded like a ragged rasp in the night. "You city girls always worry about the cattle, don't you?"

"We worry about the cowboys sometimes too," she said softly.

For an instant, he gazed at her, and even through the darkness she would swear she saw yearning in his blue eyes before he swiftly concealed his expression. "Well, the cattle and the cowboys all ought to be just fine. Tomorrow we're going to go over to Walt Stover's, just on the other side of the Triple S, to help him truck out his stock."

Without looking to see if she followed, he guided Captain from the horse trailer and into the barn. She paused outside for a moment before following him to a stall where he began grooming the black horse.

She just wanted to talk to him, she told herself. To assure herself he was fine and everything at the threatened ranches was under control.

Liar, a little voice whispered in her head. *You can't stay away from him.* Rachel shushed it, but not before she acknowledged the truth. She was drawn to him and she didn't have the energy to fight it.

She perched on a bale of straw while he picked up a brush and brushed Captain, speaking low praise for the animal's hard efforts that day. As she listened to his deep, rough voice whisper so gently, Rachel was stunned by the wave of sensation that crashed over her. With a fierce, urgent need she wanted to hear those soft words directed at her. Wanted his strong fingers to touch her with just an ounce of the affection he used on his horse.

Good heavens, how low had she sunk in life? She was actually jealous of a horse! She felt color soak her cheeks and was grateful Sam didn't look in her direction as he hefted the saddle and carried it to the tack room.

Away from the horse, the silence between them seemed to stretch and pull. Just as it became uncomfortable, Rachel blurted out the first thought that came to her. "I saw that nativity set you're making."

As soon as the words escaped her, she wanted to snatch them back. How could she possibly explain why she had been snooping around his desk? She didn't understand it herself.

He didn't comment on it, though, just looked faintly embarrassed.

"Jo's been after me for years to make her one, and I finally broke down and started it a couple weeks ago in my spare time. I wanted it to be a surprise, though."

She smiled, relieved he didn't question what she'd been doing pawing through his things. "I can keep a secret. Cross my heart."

He smiled back. "I believe you."

"It's beautiful," she said earnestly. "I especially like the angel."

To her surprise, color climbed his cheeks through the day's dark growth of stubble. "What do you mean by that?"

"I meant it's beautiful, that's all. Just what I said. What did you think I meant?"

He looked away, suddenly busy hanging tack on the pegs along the wall. "So . . . I guess you, uh, probably figured out she looks like you."

It took a moment for his words to register, and when they did, she stared at him in shock. "Wha—what?"

"Well, I couldn't help it," he snapped, and speared her with an angry glare. "I tried three times and every time the damn thing came out looking like you. I finally just gave up."

Heat and fire spread through her. Like her? Sam had carved *her?* She shot a quick glance at the table where the figurines were spread. She'd forgotten to replace the blueprint, she realized. Even at this distance, she could see the resemblance now that he'd pointed it out. No wonder the carving hadn't seemed angelic to her! It was too earthy, too sensual. Was that how he saw her?

Her heart picked up a pace and she felt her blood spill through her body like water from the Fourth of July Falls.

"Sam, I—I don't know what to say."

"Well, don't say anything," he growled. "It's not your damn fault I can't get you out of my mind. Every time I turn around, there you are yanking at me, tugging at me, until I can't think straight. Until it's all I can do not to take you right there."

With jerky movements, he tossed his Stetson onto the desk and ran a frustrated hand through hat-flattened hair. "Hell, Rachel, I want you so bad I ache with it."

His fierce words seemed to echo in the cavernous barn, and all the heat from their afternoon embrace flowed back through her. She swayed with it, with the force of the emotions in her chest, in her stomach.

Before she could think through the wisdom of her actions, she stepped toward him, until only a few feet separated them.

"I ache too, Sam," she whispered.

He stared at her, and she could see a pulse beat in his neck, could see the black of his pupils expand until it nearly crowded out the blue. And then he reached for her.

NINE

He kissed her ferociously, like a man who'd been denied food for weeks and suddenly had a sumptuous banquet laid out before him. And she relished it. She gloried in the feel of his strong arms clutching her tightly, of his hard body caressing the length of her own. She savored the taste of his mouth as it captured hers.

Finally, when she felt as if her knees wouldn't support her weight anymore, he pulled away. "I must smell like the trail."

"You smell wonderful," she admitted breathlessly.

His eyes darkened and he reached for her again. She went willingly, pressing herself against him. She couldn't seem to get close enough, and in frustration she stood on tiptoe, her arms tight around his neck. The movement pressed her breasts against the taut muscles of his chest. She wanted more of the contact, so she rubbed harder, feeling the shock of sensation as her breasts swelled and peaked.

Still kissing her, he moved to the big oak desk and boosted her up so she was perched on the edge. The position brought their bodies even closer, allowing her to cradle his thighs between hers. She gasped at the swell of his arousal, hard and insistent, pressing into her through the denim of his jeans and the cotton of her shorts. She wanted more. Much more. She wanted to feel his skin next to hers, wanted to cradle him with her hips as he drove into her.

The force of her need stunned her. Terrified her, even. She just wasn't the type of woman to blaze like this in a man's arms. Was she?

Well, apparently she was. She caught her breath as he lifted her shirt free of her shorts and slid his callused hand up her back. Rough skin on smooth. Hard against soft.

A shiver raced through her and she arched against him, pushing her hips closer, seeking something she couldn't name but knew she would find here, in his arms.

At her movement, though, Sam stiffened. He stood in her embrace for several seconds, then backed away, his face twisted with pain and need.

"This is insane," he finally said. "We can't do this, Rachel."

"Why not?" she whispered, fighting the urge to rub her hands over her shoulders at the sudden chill of being away from him.

"Because you're Rachel Lawrence and I'm nothing but a damn construction worker."

The anger in his voice scraped along her nerves. "Can't you forget that for two seconds?" she snapped.

"I'm just me. Me! A woman who slept with a night-light on until she was eighteen, who likes curling up with a good book on a rainy night, who gets angry when people mistreat kids and animals."

She paused, her blood pulsing loud and fierce in her ears, then spoke quietly. "I'm just a woman, Sam, like any other, who wants to be loved. Even if it's only for a little while."

He looked away, his expression as stony as the mountains outside the barn. "I can't handle any more of these little teasing games we've been playing. If I kiss you again, I'm not stopping."

She ought to heed that warning in his voice. Ought to just tell him good night and be on her way to the safety of her room. If she had any sense of self-preservation, that's exactly what she would do.

She opened her mouth to say the words, then shut it again. She couldn't push him away. She didn't *want* to push him away. Though she was terribly unsophisticated when it came to men and women—the sum total of her experience had been as a twenty-year-old wife— she knew what they had together was a rare and precious thing. She wouldn't give that up.

"Kiss me again, Sam," she ordered, then held her breath, praying he would. She would die if he didn't, if he walked away and left her sitting there with her soul exposed.

His jaw worked for several seconds, and she thought he would do just that—walk out of the barn— until he looked back at her, a hint of a smile playing around his firm, sensual mouth.

"Bossy, aren't you?"

"When I have to be," she retorted, still holding her breath.

"I like that in a woman."

The smile turned into a full-fledged grin, and Rachel felt as if the sun had just come out from behind years full of clouds.

He walked back to her and planted his hands on the desk at her sides. Their gazes locked, and she nearly moaned aloud at the desire gleaming in his eyes.

"I want you, Rachel Lawrence. Hard and fast, deep and slow. Any damn way I can have you."

"What are you waiting for, cowboy?" she whispered, then gasped when he yanked her hard against him and devoured her mouth.

This time there was nothing between them, just the heady sense of anticipation thrumming through her. Her senses whirling, Rachel kissed him back. When he nudged apart her lips, she welcomed him. When he slid his big, hard hands to the buttons of her shirt, she helped him slip them free, helped him work the front clasp of her bra. When his fingers brushed against her breasts, she moaned and arched into him.

His breathing harsh against her mouth, he cupped her, flicking his thumb over a nipple, teasing, coaxing it into a hard peak.

When the torment became unbearable, she straightened. With fingers that trembled, she undid the buttons of his denim work shirt, craving the feel of his skin next to hers. As each button came loose, she exposed more of the hard muscles beneath, chiseled from years of strenuous work.

He was beautiful. Rough and strong and male. She

had thought so the day she arrived, when she'd seen him working down by the barn without his shirt on. She had wanted to touch him then, had wanted to explore those muscles that flexed in the sunlight.

She remembered the stunning force of that impulse. Now, there was nothing stopping her. Rachel smiled at the realization and trailed her hands from shoulder to sternum, then back again.

He stood motionless, his heat caressing her like a warm fire on a winter's night, and she didn't want to stop. She pulled the shirt free and tossed it onto the desk, then ran her hands over his biceps, over his shoulders, down his chest again, fascinated by the tightness of his skin, by the line of hair that arrowed to the waistband of his jeans.

He made a sound low in his chest and it rumbled under her fingertips. Diverted, she glanced up and found him staring at her through hot, glittering eyes.

"No wonder I was jealous as hell every time you sat there in front of me and petted that damn cat," he murmured. "If I'd known how good it would feel to have your hands on me, I'd have tossed Nuisance onto the floor and crawled into your lap myself."

"I might have let you."

He studied her for a moment longer, then pulled her to the shadows of the big, plump couch. "Last chance, darlin'. If you want out, you have to tell me now, while I can still stop."

She shook her head and stepped forward, her cheek pressed to his chest, to the heartbeat that pulsed in her ear, fierce and loud. "Why would I want you to do a stupid thing like that?" she whispered.

He tilted his head back for a moment, staring up at the ceiling, then his hands came around and gripped her hair. She lifted her face for his kiss as he pushed her back to the couch, covering her with his body.

He trailed kisses from her mouth to her ear, down her throat, across the dips and hollows of her collarbone. She twisted her hands into his hair and gave in to the torrent of sensations.

When he reached her breasts, he paused for a moment, his breath hot on the sensitive skin until her nerves screamed with tension, with need, then he dipped his tongue around one nipple. Rachel felt as if her lungs had collapsed, as if all the air had been sucked out of the room, as if she would burn away into cinders.

She thrust her hips against him, against the hard pressure between her thighs, while he licked and teased. Finally, when she didn't think she could stand the sweet torture another instant, he slid his hand inside the waistband of her shorts, then he was cupping her. She moaned and pushed against him, needing more and more and more.

His mouth caught hers again in one of those long, drugging kisses, as he pushed one finger deep inside her, then two. She sobbed his name as he danced his thumb across the sensitive nub of flesh at the apex of her thighs, and he pushed inside her again, over and over, while his thumb stroked her.

She felt as if she were whirling and spiraling, as if they were on a wild merry-go-round, moving faster and faster, harder and harder. She shoved her hips against his hand, wild with need, until at last the merry-go-round broke away from the ground and went spinning into the air. Just before she would have flown free, he caught her with his hard, rough, wonderful hands and brought her back to earth.

She lay there, cradled by him, while her body pulsed and trembled. Finally her breathing slowed, her senses returned, and she became aware of him watching her, his face taut with need. She smiled then, the sweet, confident smile of a woman exactly where she wanted to be.

She reached for him. With quick, sure movements, he slid her shorts down over her legs, then kicked off his boots and reached for the metal buttons of his jeans.

She slid her hands to his waistband. "Let me," she whispered, and slowly worked each button free. In seconds, he was naked, and she felt her blood heat again with anticipation as he covered her with his body, skin to skin. His gaze locked with hers, and she clasped his shoulders as he slowly, carefully, sheathed himself within the heat of her body.

He groaned. "You're so tight."

"I'm sorry," she whispered, and he gave a low, ragged laugh.

"Don't apologize, darlin'. I wasn't complaining."

"Oh." She smiled back. "In that case, I'm not sorry."

This was right, Rachel thought. It had to be. With Sam, in his arms, she felt safe and warm and beautiful. He made her laugh. He made her feel alive again—

Suddenly all her thoughts scattered like thistledown on a hard October wind as he pushed inside her, sending waves of sensation rippling through her body.

"Sam!" she gasped.

"Did I hurt you?" he asked, pulling away again.

"No," she breathed. "Do that again."

"Bossy, bossy woman," he teased, but obliged her. Immediately, the merry-go-round started up again in a whirling, twirling rush.

He grabbed her hands and held them above her head, then his mouth caught hers while his body moved inside her, and she thought she would scream from the tension building within her.

Just when she thought she couldn't stand the sweet agony another moment, he reached between their bodies and flicked his fingers over the source of her fire, and the world exploded into brilliant, shiny fragments. She cried his name against his mouth. At the sound of her voice he stiffened, then he joined her.

Several minutes passed before her pulse slowed, before the room slid into focus again.

"Wow," she murmured. It didn't begin to describe the wild riot of feeling still surging through her, but since her brain wasn't completely functioning yet, it was the best she could do.

He chuckled hoarsely. "Double wow. Triple wow. Quadruple wow with ice cream on top."

She was still smiling as she drifted into sleep.

She had no idea how long they dozed there, nestled together on the big couch. When she awoke, she could see outside the little square window that the moon had set and the stars glittered alone, and she knew only warmth and softness and a sweet lassitude.

Eyes wide open, she stared at nothing and listened to the steady thump of his heartbeat. It had been so long, so terribly long, since she'd experienced this closeness with another person. She'd missed it, she realized. Not the actual physical act of making love as much as the intimacy of it, the complete and total connection two people shared.

She smiled slightly. Sam had been tender and sweet, so unlike the gruff cowboy she'd imagined him to be. He had whispered how beautiful she was, how he was afraid of hurting her. The whole time she had wanted to wrap her arms around those powerful shoulders of his and hold on forever.

The urge startled her. She still wanted to. Rachel stiffened, her contentment fading as common sense intruded.

What had she done? She'd let down the tight guard she kept around her heart, and when she wasn't looking Sam had somehow slipped inside. Now she felt exposed, painfully vulnerable.

How could she have been so stupid? And how could she possibly return to her quiet little cottage now, to the sterile coldness that had filled her life for the past five years, when she'd been exposed to the wonder and magic and sunlight she'd found in Sam's arms?

Not just in his arms, she had to admit. In his home, with his sons. Back here in Whiskey Creek, of all places, she'd found happiness for the first time in years.

"What put that frown on your face? Not me, I hope."

She started, not realizing he'd awakened. She shifted her gaze to his lean face and found him gazing at her with watchful blue eyes. Embarrassed heat poured through her.

"I—I was just thinking we probably shouldn't have done this."

He made a low sound that rumbled under her ear. "You ever been in the middle of a fast-moving Type One forest fire?"

She shook her head. "Of course not."

"Well, I have. There comes a time, darlin', when you know there's not one damn thing you can do to slow it down. It's too strong for anybody to fight it. You just have to ride it out or get the hell out of the way."

He paused, then lifted a hand to her cheek. "This thing between us, whatever you want to call it, is definitely at least a Type One."

Despite her emotional tumult, she laughed and leaned into his hand. Her worries could wait, she decided. "Trust you, Sam Wyatt, to come up with a fire analogy at a moment like this."

"Yeah, well, you know what they say about firemen." He gave her a look that was nothing short of a leer.

"No," she played along. "What do they say?"

"They're always hot and ready for anything."

"Is that so?"

"Damn right," he said, and proceeded to demonstrate.

It was still a couple of hours before dawn when they hurried back to the house, sneaking in furtively like teenagers home late after a dance. She caught a glimpse of Sam carrying his boots so they didn't pound on the hardwood floor, and had to fight down a laugh.

"You want Josie out here investigating what the

Sam Hill we're doin' coming in at four in the morning?" he whispered.

She shook her head. "She'd probably kick me from here to Pinedale for corrupting your morals."

He gave a low laugh. "Yeah, I was as pure as a newborn lamb before you came along."

He pulled her close for another of those long, sexy kisses. After a few heady moments, he leaned back. "My morals could use a little more corrupting," he murmured. "Sure I can't convince you to have your wicked way with me again?"

If she had her wicked way, she'd curl up against him and not let go, but she knew they would both be exhausted if she did.

"You need to sleep," she said. "It's been a long day for you, and I wouldn't want you to fall asleep in your saddle tomorrow while you're on roundup."

He studied her for several seconds, then tucked her hair behind her ear and kissed her gently, sweetly, on the forehead. "I know damn well I shouldn't, Rachel, but I like you worrying about me. Watching out for me." He caressed her cheek, then turned and walked down the hall to his room.

He was the biggest fool this side of the Rockies.

Sam drove his pickup into the Elkhorn driveway about an hour after sunset and watched the house warily. Pounding the trails that day looking for Walt Stover's stray calves had given him nothing but time to think. To remember in excruciating detail the soft, warm expanse of Rachel's skin, how she'd welcomed him into her arms and her body like he belonged there. To relive the moments when he'd died in her arms.

And time to fret and stew about this moment when he would have to face her again.

He wanted nothing more than to go to her and crawl back into the wonder and magic they found together. Through a long day of gnawing on it, though, he'd come to realize what a dumb idea that would be. She wasn't sticking around and it was senseless to let this go any further. What would come of it, anyway? It was only a matter of time before she left.

Hell, maybe she was already gone. A bleak devastation, like a killing November frost, swept over him and nearly took his breath away. Maybe she'd already taken her sweet laughter and her gentleness and gone back to where she belonged, to her high-society life.

He clenched his jaw. What did it matter to him? She didn't belong here anyway, not with those smooth hands and her frail bones and her delicate features.

His movements jerky, he hurriedly groomed Captain and let him into the pasture with water and oats, then walked up to the house. By the time he rounded the corner, he'd just about convinced himself she had returned to Santa Barbara.

When he spied her sitting on the wide front porch, calmly swaying back and forth on Jo's big rocking chair, Nuisance cuddled comfortably on her lap, he stopped stock-still. That was surprise gushing through him, he told himself. It couldn't be relief he felt at seeing her looking sleek and elegant and *right* on his porch.

"Hi," she said cheerfully.

He mumbled a greeting and walked to the steps, unsure how to act, how to treat her, and hating himself for it.

"We didn't know when to expect you. Have you eaten?"

"No. I had a sandwich for lunch, though."

"You're probably starving, then. Your dinner is on a plate in the refrigerator. I can throw it in the microwave for you while you wash up, if you'd like."

"Thanks," he mumbled, still not meeting her gaze.

He tried to ignore the swell of his body. Dammit. Damn *her*. All he wanted to do was grab her and take her right there on the porch. Instead, he followed her into the house.

"Where is everybody?"

"Asleep. The boys begged and pleaded to stay up until you came back, but I thought it would be better for them to stick to their regular schedules. They've been wired all day with all this excitement around."

"Jo?"

"She's down too. I heard her television set on a while ago, but I think she finally turned in."

We're alone. She didn't say the words, but they seemed to linger in the air anyway, haunting him with the implications.

Sam gripped the pine railing on the stairs. *You decided this wasn't smart, letting this thing go on anymore*, he reminded himself.

All his good intentions sure were hard to remember, though, with her looking so happy to see him, with that smile on her face and her beautiful gray eyes lit up like it was her birthday or something.

Of course, as soon as she found out what he planned to do in the morning, he knew that smile would die quicker than a garden in the middle of a drought.

"Think I'll take a shower before I eat," he muttered, and headed up the stairs without looking back. A nice long, cold shower might be just the thing he needed to keep his mind off of last night, off the heat and fire of her arms and her body.

Who you kiddin', Wyatt? A hundred years of cold showers wouldn't be enough to wipe out those memories.

Sure enough, he was still uncomfortably aroused when he walked downstairs in clean jeans and a fresh shirt, with his hair wet and at least some of his exhaustion washed away.

She gave him a sweet smile as he walked into the kitchen, then she pulled a huge plate of lasagna out of the microwave. It smelled divine, but not nearly as good as the woman standing there offering it to him.

While he ate, she sat with him at the table and chattered on about everything: the progress the boys were making on that treehouse they were putting together, the fish Noah caught that evening at the pond, a story Jo told her.

It was too comfortable, he thought. Too domestic. Like a wife telling her husband about her day. Lord, he'd missed this.

In the years since Hannah's death, he'd been too busy with the boys and the ranch and the construction business to dwell on the thousands of little things he missed about her, about the three short years they'd had together before a drunk cowboy in a pickup had stolen her from him in that accident.

If he hadn't been so overwhelmed doing everything on his own and coping with his grief, he knew this would have been near the top of the list, this slow, easy intimacy that had nothing to do with sex.

The knowledge that Rachel could bring back all those feelings that had died with Hannah scared the hell out of him. He could feel her tugging at him, drawing him closer to her, and knew he was asking for nothing but trouble to let it go any further.

Tell her now, he thought, but couldn't make himself form the words. It was cowardly of him, he knew, but he couldn't stand the idea of that warm expression on her face fading to hurt and anger when she found out where he planned to be in the morning.

He frowned. She *wasn't* his wife, and he'd do well to remember that. He didn't owe her any explanations. Didn't owe her anything. He swore, then stood abruptly and crossed to the sink to rinse his plate. When he turned, she was watching him carefully.

"Thanks for dinner," he muttered. "Guess I better turn in."

"You want to tell me what I did this time?"

"You didn't do anything." *Except sit there looking so soft and warm and beautiful it's all I can do to keep myself away from you.*

"I see. So is this a Whiskey Creek custom I don't know about? Some way of signaling you're done with your meal? You swear up a blue streak right in the middle of a conversation and then jump up and walk away?"

He grimaced at his rudeness. "Sorry," he mumbled. "This is about last night, isn't it?"

He should just end it right there. A few simple words was all it would take and she would be eager to push him away.

"Look, Rachel," he began, then stumbled over his thoughts when she uncoiled gracefully from the chair and crossed to him, placing a long finger on his lips.

"Don't, Sam."

"Rachel—"

"I don't want to hear about all the reasons you think last night was a mistake. You're probably right, but I can't regret it. I won't regret it. I'm sorry, Sam."

He closed his eyes, still feeling the softness of her skin on his lips. He couldn't regret making love to her either, as much as he'd like to.

"What do you want from me, Rachel?"

"Whatever you're willing to give," she said simply.

Sam studied her, his jaw working, then he cursed again and reached for her.

TEN

She tasted like heaven, a tropical, exotic heaven, and he felt his senses spin just being close to her. He pressed her against the sink, as he'd done that first night they'd kissed here. She molded herself to him, her arms tight around his waist, and gave a soft, breathy sigh of pleasure that rocketed straight to his gut.

"How do you do that?" he growled.

"Do what?"

"I've spent the last ten hours telling myself we shouldn't do this again. Damned if I can remember all the reasons why not when you're here next to me."

"Don't try," she said softly.

"Rachel—" He needed to tell her now, before he completely lost his resolve. But as he looked at her, sweetly vulnerable in the dimly lit kitchen, he couldn't come up with the words.

She took the decision out of his hands when she stepped forward and offered herself to him again, her face lifted for his kiss like a sun-starved flower reaching for the sky.

Sam sighed in resignation. He wanted her. Hell, he *needed* her. If she wanted him, too, how could he turn her away?

"No regrets, Rachel. Promise me that in the morning you won't be sorry."

"Cross my heart," she whispered.

He pulled her into his arms for another of her intoxicating kisses. It was unbearably arousing, the way she melted in his arms like this. He licked and teased his way across her mouth and was working free the buttons on her shirt when he heard the muted creak of bedsprings from Josie's room.

He froze for several seconds, then refastened her buttons carefully. "Maybe we ought to take this somewhere we won't be interrupted."

"My room has a nice big bed."

He grinned. "Mine's bigger."

"Now why do I get the feeling you say that to all the girls?" she teased.

Instantly, he sobered. "I've never had a woman in the house before, Rachel. Never wanted to."

It seemed important, somehow, that she understand what a huge step this was for him. Hannah had been dead more than six years and he would have been lying if he'd said he hadn't been with any women since then. But he'd never felt strongly enough about any of them to bring them here, to his home, to his bed.

She studied him for a moment, then nodded and reached out a hand. With anticipation boiling through his blood, he clasped her fingers and tugged her up-stairs.

Kicking his door shut, he guided her toward the huge log bed. The only light in the room came from the full moon, but it was enough for him to again be astonished by her beauty as he unwrapped the few layers of clothes covering her.

It wasn't just her physical beauty that pulled him to her. It was that serenity she seemed to exude, the gentle care she'd given to everyone at the ranch since she'd been there.

He was especially touched by the way she interacted with the boys, the changes he'd seen in both of them since she'd come. Zach used to be so serious all the time, had tried so hard to keep his feelings locked away. It had worried him, he admitted. Since she arrived, though, he'd begun acting more like a nine-year-old ought to. Building that treehouse, wading in the pond. Just having fun being a kid. Noah, too, had bloomed under Rachel's attention, becoming less prone to tantrums and snits when things didn't go his way.

She had brought out the best in all of them, he realized. When she drove away, he was very much afraid she would leave a void in their lives that no one else would be able to fill.

Sam shoved aside the thought. He didn't want to worry about her leaving. Not tonight.

He gave in to impulse and kissed the delicate hollow in her neck, then the bones in her wrists, then the curve of her jaw. With each touch of his mouth on her skin, she gave a tiny shiver, and the visible signs of her heightened desire were almost more than he could handle.

Last night, he'd been too close to the edge after two weeks of near-constant arousal to savor the sheer sensory overload of having her in his arms. Tonight, he would take his time. He would explore every single inch of her soft skin, would memorize every response. It might be the last time she would be in his arms and he wanted it to last forever.

He tried. Damned if he didn't try. He kissed her mouth, her neck, her breasts, for what felt like hours. He glided down that long, sexy length of her legs, then worked his way back up. He made it as far as the curve of her hip before his body began to shake with need.

He tried to ignore it, but Rachel seemed to sense his growing torment, the passion he thought would burst inside him, because she reached for him. At the feel of her fingers around him, he nearly splintered apart, but she guided him inside her silken depths.

Every muscle straining with the need to surge into her, he held himself as still as he could. Their gazes locked as his mouth descended, and she met his kiss with eager abandon.

She writhed and twisted beneath him, seeking fulfillment. Her breathing was as ragged as his, and her hands caressed him greedily, as if she couldn't get enough of him.

When he thought he couldn't stand it another second, he finally sank deep inside her, murmuring soft words against her mouth. She seemed to climax immediately, coming apart in a soft, liquid rush, her body arched beneath him like a bowstring.

At the feel of her pulsing around him, he could hold on to his control no longer. He groaned her name, then with one powerful thrust the world exploded in a blinding flash of light and heat.

She snuggled into him, her arms around his bare torso, and he could swear he felt her smile against his skin before the exhaustion of the day finally claimed him.

Rachel held him while he slept, loathe to give up these precious remaining moments with him. He looked so relaxed in sleep. Younger, somehow. A lock of dark hair slipped down over his eyes and she fought a powerful urge to tuck it back. Just before she reached for it, she forced her hand to fall again to his chest. He needed his sleep and she didn't want to take the risk of awakening him.

Rachel inhaled a breath that sounded like a sob. He was stubborn and arrogant and exasperating, and she was so deeply in love with him, she didn't know if she'd ever be able to climb out.

She lay there for a long time listening to his heartbeat before she finally surrendered to sleep.

When she awoke, the morning sun shone through the windows. She was alone, she realized, tangled in the sheets that smelled of him. She inhaled deeply, then reached a hand out and touched the pillow that still bore the imprint from his head.

She wanted to stay there the rest of the day, but she knew Josie and the boys would be wondering about her, so she forced herself to climb out of bed, to leave the soft sanctuary they'd created the night before.

The boys were eating breakfast when she descended the stairs a short time later.

" 'Morning, Aunt Rachel," Zach said. "Grandma made pancakes and there's tons more."

Rachel glanced at Josie, standing by the stove with a spatula in her hand, healthy and vigorous once again. For an instant her heart seemed to crumple in her chest. She had no reason to stay anymore, not with Josie assuming all her old duties. No reason at all, except she didn't want to be anywhere else.

"Dad ate seven whole pancakes before he left," Noah said proudly. "Said he was starvin' right to death."

Though a lump swelled in her throat and her eyes suddenly burned, Rachel summoned a smile and rubbed his hair. "They certainly smell delicious. You'd better get cooking, Josie. Maybe I'll have to eat seven whole pancakes too."

The boy giggled. "Maybe you and Dad could have a pancake-eatin' contest. Betcha a dollar he'd win," Noah said.

Rachel smiled and reached into the cupboard for another plate. "So where is your dad this morning?"

She wanted the question to come out casually, but Josie aimed a sharp, piercing look at her.

Both boys shrugged. "Don't know," Zach said. "He just gave us hugs and said he'd be back as soon as he could."

"Is he out on roundup again, Jo?"

"Nope. Not this time." Josie suddenly seemed inordinately busy at the stove. "If you boys are done playin' with your food, go on down and make sure your dad fed the dogs before he left."

Both boys, always eager to be outside, slid their chairs back and left after quick hugs to Rachel. If she held them a little longer than completely necessary and rubbed her cheek against their hair, well, they didn't seem to see anything unusual in it.

"So where did you say Sam went?" she asked when the two women were alone in the kitchen.

Josie studied her for a long moment, her brown eyes murky and troubled. "You might as well know. He's gone out on that fire."

Rachel stared, her blood suddenly pounding through her veins. She swayed, then gripped the slats of a kitchen chair to help her regain equilibrium. "He—he what?"

"Said he likely wouldn't be much help, but he had to do what he could. Not on the fire line itself, just workin' at the base camp. Radio communications or some fancy name like that."

It made her feel slightly better that he wasn't directly in the path of the fire, but not much. "When? Did he tell you when he decided to do this?"

Josie shrugged. "Don't know when, exactly. I think it was last night. Turns out the fire boss on the Big Muddy complex used to work with him in the forest service. He tracked Sam down at Walt's place yesterday and told him they were comin' up short on men. He told Sam to get off his butt and help 'em out there, so he did."

Last night. He'd known last night—when he'd been

in her arms, inside her body—that he would be leaving in the morning. "I . . . I see."

All her foolish dreams seemed to shatter into shards of glass around her feet. If she'd needed any more proof that her feelings were completely one-sided, here it was. If he cared about her, even a little, he would have told her he was going out on the fire.

No, she corrected herself. If he cared about her, he wouldn't have even considered fighting the fire, not when he knew how fiercely she hated and feared it.

"Jo, I don't think I'm hungry after all. I need to make a phone call."

She didn't wait for an answer, just rushed out of the kitchen.

"If you'd called an hour ago, Ms. Lawrence, we could have squeezed you onto one of our later flights. But it seems everyone's leaving because of the fires. All of our flights are completely booked until tomorrow afternoon at the earliest."

Rachel nearly moaned aloud in frustration at the reservation clerk's answer. She wanted out now, before Sam returned, not tomorrow afternoon. Since she'd made the decision to return to California, she wasn't emotionally prepared for any further delays.

"I see," she finally said. "Well, book me on the earliest possible flight, then."

"That would be with a five-thirty P.M. departure time from the airport in Jackson Hole to Los Angeles International, then a short connector flight to Santa Barbara."

"Fine." She quickly gave her credit card number and wrote down the flight information. Another thirty-six hours, give or take a few, and she would be home, once again back in the safety of her life.

She hung up the phone and turned to find Josie had followed her into the family room. The older woman watched her out of those brown eyes that seemed to miss nothing.

"It's long past time I returned," Rachel said quietly, trying to keep any defensiveness out of her voice. "You seem to be fine now, so there's really no reason for me to stay."

"Guess you're right. Still, I'd hoped maybe you'd decide to stick around a little longer. Take care of all your unfinished business."

"What unfinished business?"

"Sam."

"What—what do you mean?"

"You care about that boy. I can see it every time you two get together. The two of you put out more heat than a dozen Big Muddy fires."

Oh mercy. Had she been that obvious? She thought she'd been able to hide her burgeoning feelings. She'd even concealed them from herself for most of her time there, hadn't she? Apparently she hadn't been successful if Jo could read her so easily.

"I don't know what to say."

"What's there to say? It's none of my business, anyway, though I won't lie to you, I'd be tickled to death if the two of you did get together."

"You—you would?"

Josie's face softened, the normally harsh lines easing into a small, romantic smile. " 'Course I would. Thought for a while there you had somethin' goin', the way you blushed redder'n that barn out back whenever he walked in and the way he couldn't seem to keep his eyes off you."

Rachel flushed, trying to assimilate this new information. "Josie," she began, but the older woman interrupted her with a shrug.

"I tried to milk this blasted pneumonia thing as long as I could, hopin' the two of you would finally wise up, but I just couldn't stand that room another minute. Guess I was wrong about it all, anyway, if you're leavin' tomorrow."

Why, the old sneak! Pretending to be sick to give her and Sam time to develop their feelings for each other! She remembered now the evasiveness of the last several days. Jo never wanted to talk about how she was feeling and she promptly changed the subject whenever the topic came up.

Rachel didn't know whether to laugh or be angry at the older woman's deviousness. "But Doc Matthews. He said you needed bed rest."

Josie busied herself with a dusting rag. "I did, at first. He just kinda bluffed for the last week or so. I had to promise I'd let him take me to the weddin' if it worked out." Jo grinned, and for an instant Rachel saw the feisty young woman inside her, despite her seventy-some years. "That old goat's been tryin' to get inside my bloomers for years."

"Josie!"

"Well, he has." Color bloomed on her sun-weathered cheeks, and Rachel had to smile, despite her lingering shock. Josie and Seth Matthews. They made a perfect pair. She and Sam, on the other hand . . .

"But why?" she finally said. "Why would you think Sam and I . . . That is . . ." Her voice trailed off. "I was married to your son, for heaven's sake. Doesn't that bother you?"

Josie's smile turned bittersweet. "I was married for twenty-five years to the best darn husband around. The worst rancher, mind ya, but you couldn't find a better man. When Bill died of that heart attack, for a long time I wanted to die too. But you have to go on."

She touched Rachel's hand. "I know you loved my Matt, but you can't hide inside that for the rest of yer life. If you got a chance to find somethin' like that again, I'd be the first one to tell ya you'd be a damn fool to throw it away."

"Oh, Josie."

She battled her emotions, wishing more than anything that she could lay her head on the other woman's bony shoulder and indulge in a good, long cry. What a tangled mess everything had become.

"Besides," Jo went on briskly, "Sam's a good, decent man who's worked mighty hard to save this ranch. He deserves a bit of sunshine in his life, somebody to make him smile again. And those boys need a mother, that's God's honest truth. I do what I can, but I'm gettin' older and I just can't keep up with 'em like I used to."

She paused, as if to let her words sink in. "I've never seen any of 'em happier than these few weeks you've been here."

Rachel felt the crack in her heart widen even more. "I can't stay, Jo. Surely you can see that."

Jo nodded sadly. "You do what you have to, girl."

After packing her things, Rachel tried to spend as much of her remaining time as she could with Zach and Noah. She didn't want to tell them she was leaving the next day, not and ruin their last few hours together, so she forced a cheerful smile and helped them work on the treehouse down by the horse pasture.

She was perched on a sturdy branch hammering a board to one of the flimsy walls when Jo appeared.

"Think you could run into town for me and take this cooler full of potato salad to the church? Some of the ladies have a relief effort goin' and I promised I'd do my share."

"A relief effort?" Rachel swung to the ground, her heart racing as her mind conjured up images of bandaged, scarred firefighters. "For what? There aren't injuries, are there?"

"Oh, no, nothin' like that. This is for food. Them men up there are all sick and tired of eatin' those packaged meals the forest service gives out, the same nasty things the army gives soldiers in the middle of a war. From what Matt and Sam used to say, I gather you only eat 'em if you're starvin' right to death. Usually the forest service hires some fancy caterer, but they're having a hard time gettin' any in with all the other fires in the area, so a bunch of women in town are puttin' some good ol' western grub together to show their appreciation."

The last thing she wanted to do on her final evening there was face the women of Whiskey Creek again. She had no doubts Karen Peters would be involved in this care effort up to her nosy little eyeballs, and Rachel simply didn't know if she had the emotional strength for another run-in with the woman.

"So can you take it into Whiskey Creek?" Jo asked again. "I don't drive so well at night, and it's gonna be dark in another hour or so."

With an inward sigh, Rachel tossed the hammer into the motley pile of nails and boards the boys had scrounged from their father. She didn't want to go, but it looked as if she didn't have any kind of choice in the matter. Josie could be as tenacious as her son-in-law.

"Of course, Josie," she finally said. "Just let me wash up."

On second thought, maybe it wouldn't be such a bad idea. She needed something to keep her busy, to keep her mind from dwelling on tomorrow afternoon, when she would be flying away from Wyoming and the joy she'd found here.

He'd forgotten it all. Forgotten the heat and the smoke and the exhaustion that never seemed to end. And he'd forgotten the exhilaration. The bizarre adrenaline rush pumping through him at the elemental battle of man against nature.

Even in the base camp command center, more than a mile away from any flames, the mood was tense, stressful, and completely invigorating.

Just like climbing back on a horse after you've been bucked off, Sam thought. All the motions and the words and the procedures came flowing back the minute he walked into camp, and he hadn't missed a beat.

"You're doin' great."

Sam glanced up at Charlie McBride, the fire boss. "Not too bad for a guy who hasn't seen a fire bigger than his woodstove in five years now."

"Not bad at all." Charlie grinned at him just as a kid who couldn't be more than twenty poked his head through the doorway of the command center tent.

"Dinner's here," the new arrival said. "And man, did they get some hot-lookin' lady to bring it out. She's gotta be pretty brave to face a camp full of lonely, horny firefighters." He winked. "You all want me to bring you back some?"

"Some of the dinner or some of the lady?" Charlie grinned, and the other firefighters laughed.

Sam stood. If it was one of the Whiskey Creek women out there, she might not know how to handle the raw teasing that could go on in a fire camp. He'd just go give her a hand, he decided. Help deflect a little of the more persistent attention.

"Mind if I take a break, Charlie? I need to stretch my legs a bit. Maybe I'll go help Junior out there."

The fire boss nodded, and Sam walked out into the evening air. It was close to dusk, and with all the particulates in the air from the vast fire, the sunset was incredible. Mauves and purples and flame-orange streaks painted the sky above the mountains.

He was so busy looking at the sight he didn't pay much attention to anything else until he rounded a row of tents. Suddenly he stopped in his tracks and stared. If he didn't know better, he would swear that was the other Elkhorn pickup, the one Josie used to pick up supplies from town. What the hell was that doing here?

A half-dozen firefighters ringed the tailgate of the pickup. As he watched, a slender woman bent over to reach into the back of the truck and pull out something she handed to one of the men.

Rachel. He could tell instantly, even before he was close enough to make out her features.

Did he really know her that well? Could he recognize her simply by the curve of a hip and the graceful tilt of her neck?

Yeah. He could. Damn her. Didn't she have enough sense to realize driving out to a fire camp wasn't a nice little cruise through the country? And what was Jo thinking to let her come out here? He frowned and picked up his pace, until he was nearly running.

He plowed through the barrier of sweaty firefighters and grabbed her by the arm. "What the hell are you doing here, Rachel?"

She jerked her gaze to his. "Sam!"

He forced himself not to feel a small flutter of pleasure at the wealth of relief and something that looked suspiciously like joy sifting through those smoky gray eyes. She looked as if she wanted to fling her arms around his neck and hold on tight forever.

Yeah, and if you believe that, Wyatt, I've got a nice little seaside cottage down by Laramie you might be interested in buying, a snide voice inside his head whispered.

"What are you doing here?" he repeated.

She shrugged. "Somebody had to bring all this food out here." She leaned back inside the pickup. He wasn't the only one aware of the way she filled out her old jeans, he noticed, and glared fiercely at every single one of the men so avidly watching her.

She's mine.

It was an unspoken warning between him and all those young bucks. They seemed to get the message loud and clear, because a few of them averted their eyes from her enticing rear end and gave him apologetic looks.

He grabbed a box from her and handed it to another firefighter. "Yeah, somebody had to bring it out here. But why did it have to be you?"

"Nobody else volunteered," she said simply.

Only then did he notice that her hands were shaking, how pale she appeared, the veneer of composure that looked as if it was about to crack.

He swore softly under his breath. She was close to the breaking point. He didn't know if it was from fear of the fire danger, from the strain of driving fifteen miles on a mountainous road to the fire camp, or just from the effort it must have taken for her to face her past, the part of her husband's life she had hated so much.

It didn't matter, really. The only important thing was, there was no way in hell he was going to let her drive back along that road at night, not in this condition.

ELEVEN

With a muttered curse, Sam grabbed another cooler from her.

"Sit down, Rachel," he ordered harshly. "Before you fall over."

"I'm fine." Despite her assurances, her hands fumbled with a large covered plastic bowl filled with what looked like Annabel Garfield's delectable dinner rolls, and she nearly dropped it.

He snatched the bowl out of her hand and stared her down. "Go back inside that truck, turn on the air conditioner, and wait for me."

His steely command finally pierced through her shaky control, because she nodded and obeyed him. He unloaded the rest of the coolers and containers of food, handing them to the other firefighters to take to the picnic tables set up in the center of camp.

Questions pounded through him as he opened the passenger-side door and climbed inside the cab of the truck. Cold air from the air conditioner soaked through him like a spring breeze. For an instant, he savored it, free of the crushing heat for the first time all day, then he turned and scowled at Rachel. She was sitting behind the steering wheel with her arms folded tightly together as if the cool air that felt so wonderful to him was freezing the blood in her veins.

"How did you end up out here?"

"I told you. No one else volunteered to bring the food out. One of the sheriff's deputies was supposed to deliver it all, but apparently he was called out on an accident at the last minute."

"Yeah, but how did you get involved?"

"Jo asked me to take her truck and drive the food she'd prepared into Whiskey Creek. When I arrived at the church where they gathered with the donations of food, I found all those women in a panic about how to bring it out here."

She gave a self-satisfied smile, the first easing of the tension he'd seen in her since he found her. "You should have seen them, Sam. All those women, Karen Peters and her crowd. Scared to death to drive fifteen measly miles. I suppose it's fairly petty of me to be so proud of myself, but I had the guts to do something they didn't. You have no idea how good that makes me feel."

"Guts or not, it was a damn stupid thing to do and I can't believe anybody let you do it in the first place. You don't know these roads, Rachel. Did it ever occur to you that you could have accidentally driven straight into the path of the fire?"

"I'm not as helpless as you seem to think. I'm here, aren't I?"

"Yeah, but you sure don't look like you're in any shape to drive back to the Elkhorn. Not in the dark, anyway."

For a moment she leaned her head back against the seat, her eyes closed as if she didn't have the energy to keep them open. "I'll be fine," she said after a moment, exhaustion threading through her voice. "Once I rest for a while, I'll be just fine."

"You'll be just fine sleeping in my tent for the night. I'll drive you back in the morning. They can do without me for a few hours."

She opened her eyes and speared him with a gray gaze. "Can they?"

The bitterness in her voice surprised him. "Rachel—"

"Why didn't you tell me last night you were coming here? Coming out to fight the fire?" Her words were so quiet he barely heard them over the fan of the cooling system.

Guilt washed through him as he had a quick vision of taking her the night before, losing himself in the haven of her body when he knew he would be leaving in the morning.

"I knew you'd be furious," he answered honestly. "I knew you'd try to convince me not to go."

She lifted an eyebrow. "Let me get this straight. You're not afraid of a few flames, a little smoke inhalation, but you chickened out when it came to telling me about it."

"I didn't chicken out," he said, stung. "I just didn't know how to tell you."

She stared straight ahead, at the bustle of activity in

the fire camp. "How about, 'It's been a barrel of laughs, sweetheart, but now I'm off to play hero. Don't wait up'? That probably would have done it."

He laughed, a low and ragged sound in the cab of the truck. "Why didn't I think of that?"

She shrugged. "You don't owe me any explanations anyway. I was just surprised to find you gone this morning."

Surprised and hurt. He didn't need her to spell it out—he could hear the pain in her voice and knew he was the cause.

"You're right. I should have told you." He fumbled for words, wishing he knew what to say, how to ease that pain. "You were just so soft and warm and you cuddled up to me last night like you couldn't stand to be away from me. I haven't . . . I haven't had that in a long time and I didn't want to ruin it. It was selfish and thoughtless of me, I knew it then. But I still couldn't bring myself to say the words. I'm sorry."

"Oh, Sam." When she lifted her gaze to his, her eyes shimmered like silver in the sun.

With a muffled groan, he reached across the truck and pulled her to him. He tasted desperation in her kiss and knew she was leaving. The knowledge plowed into him like a tornado, twisting and shaking around his insides.

How could he let her go? And how could he possibly ask her to stay?

He cupped her face and slowed the pace of their kiss, savoring each taste of her, each shivering response, storing it away for the time when she would be gone.

When he pulled away, both of them were breathing hard. Catcalls intruded from outside their air-conditioned oasis, and he glanced up to see they'd attracted a crowd. He pulled her pink face against his chest and glowered at the other firefighters, who laughed good-naturedly and moved away.

He tightened his hold. "I don't want you to leave tonight, Rachel. For my own peace of mind."

She looked up at him, and he could see indecision clouding the edges of her eyes. Finally, she nodded.

"Let's go call Josie and tell her you won't be home until morning," he said, then pulled the keys from the ignition and shoved them into his shirt pocket. "You can have these back after you've had a good night's rest and put some food in your stomach."

"Kidnapping's against the law, Wyatt," she said mildly.

He grinned, more relieved than he cared to admit that he'd at least have one more night with her. "Yeah? So sue me."

Never in a million years would Rachel have imagined herself in the middle of a fire camp.

When they walked into the clearing where two dozen folding picnic tables had been set up, Sam immediately grabbed her hand, as if to stake his claim on her.

Despite her protests—the food was for the firefighters, after all, and she didn't think her stomach could handle so much as a swallow—he insisted on filling a plate for her and ushered her to an empty table, away from the rest of the crowd.

Rachel just wanted to collapse. She'd had no idea her impetuous decision to drive the food out would be so draining, emotionally and physically. If she'd been thinking at all about anything but besting Karen Peters, she would have realized how difficult it would be.

The drive itself hadn't been arduous. The way had been clearly marked, the unpaved mountain road relatively smooth. The trucks and bulldozers and other heavy equipment being used to fight the fire must have graded it as they'd been brought to the fire camp.

As she neared the blaze burning in the distance, though, she'd felt as if she were inching closer and closer to her past. Walking back through time. This was what had taken Matt from her. Fire had been his mistress, the demanding, exciting woman he refused to give up.

She thought she was over it, that she had learned to deal with it all in the five years since he'd died. But it was taking Sam away, too, and that seemed even harder to bear.

Not that Sam had been hers to begin with, she reminded herself. Their few shared moments had likely been a mistake that would haunt her for the rest of her life.

Still, as she'd told him the night before, she couldn't regret it. Sam had given her so much these last few weeks, especially a precious store of memories she could take out and sift through when she was alone again.

After a sip of icy soda, she felt her nerves begin to

steady, and she took the chance to glance around her surroundings. It smelled of burning timber, of course, but also the sweetness of pine, the tartness of sagebrush, the sharpness of sweat. In the distance, she could see an orange glow from the fire, and if she listened hard, she could hear it crackle and hiss.

She ought to be terrified, but she was familiar enough with fire camp procedure from those few short months being married to Matt to know the camps would only be set up in a completely safe place. She would find no danger here from the flames, just from one particular stubborn, blue-eyed firefighter.

Most of the men and women at the tables in their fire-resistant yellow Nomex uniforms looked like they were barely college-age. Some of their faces were smudged with soot, some were cleaner, but the same exhaustion showed on all of them.

Rachel sipped at her soda. She was just feeling human again when two men walked into the circle of tables. Immediately, she could tell they were different from the others. It wasn't just that they were older than most of the firefighters, they just seemed to exude a tangible air of experience, of command.

One of the men, like Sam, was dressed in civilian clothes, but he also wore a black vest that said "IC" in red letters on the back.

He nudged his companion, dressed in the same bulky uniform as the other firefighters, and pointed at Sam and Rachel. As soon as they'd made it through the food line, they stopped at their table.

"Who's the woman, Wyatt?" The question from

the younger man was accompanied by a grin she could barely see under the fringe of a huge dark mustache.

"Get your own girl, Perez," Sam drawled.

"I'd like to. This one."

Rachel laughed as the man waggled his bushy eyebrows in an exaggerated leer at her.

"Don't let yourself be taken in by a pretty face, darlin'," Sam warned her. "These two are nothing but trouble."

"Then the three of you ought to get along like fleas on a dog," she said, earning hearty laughs from both of the men, who promptly sat down at the table.

The one with the mustache thrust a beefy hand in her direction. "Gabe Perez. This homely looking fellow is Charlie McBride, our esteemed incident commander."

Ah. That explained the letters on his vest, she thought. IC—Incident Commander.

"I'm Rachel Lawrence."

Sam gestured to their plates. "She's the one who brought out all this food to save your sorry hides from a mutiny if you had to feed MREs to your crew for one more meal."

The two men gave her appreciative glances. "Buy the lady a drink," the lean, graying fire boss said. "My stomach thanks you, ma'am."

Rachel smiled. "I'm afraid I didn't fix any of it. You can thank the women of Whiskey Creek for that. I'm just the delivery girl." Suddenly she felt worlds better, as if her anxieties had slipped away in the presence of all this male exuberance.

"So what's a pretty lady like you doing sitting here with this ugly flame sucker?" Gabe asked.

"She's playing with her food, thinking I'm not paying attention," Sam answered mildly. "Eat, Rachel."

She glared at him, but scooped a piece of pasta onto her fork and made a big show of popping it into her mouth.

"Beautiful and obedient too," Gabe said, with a wink at Rachel. "The perfect woman."

Sam snorted. "Right. Rachel's middle name is Stubborn. She does exactly what she wants, to hell with the consequences."

"I guess we're more alike than I thought," she said.

The other two men laughed. "She's got you there, Wyatt. The pot calling the kettle black," Gabe said.

"So how long have the three of you known each other?" Rachel asked, charmed by the two men.

"Since the first time he picked up a Pulaski," Charlie said, grinning. "Boy, he was a green kid. More muscle than smarts in those days."

The fire boss leaned his elbow on the table. "You should have seen him on that first fire we were on together. It was somewhere in Nevada, if I remember right."

"Colorado," Sam interjected. "Durango way. Do we really have to talk about this?"

"Oh. That's right. Durango. And yeah, we do." Charlie turned back to Rachel. "You should have seen him, ma'am. Eager as hell—er, heck—to get out on the fire the first day we're out there, so what do you think he did?"

The fire boss was barely holding back what promised to be a huge belly laugh, while Rachel watched the tips of Sam's ears begin to turn pink.

"Drop it, McBride," Sam growled.

Charlie ignored him. "He probably wasn't out there longer than an hour and we were all working on building a fire line. One minute he's digging along just like the rest of us, the next his face turned whiter than North Dakota in January. He kept right on workin', though, like nothing had happened, and it wasn't until later that night when he couldn't get his boot off that we all found out what happened."

"What?"

Charlie grinned, savoring the punch line, but Sam stole his glory.

"I broke two of my toes, okay? I stuck the damn shovel through my boot and broke my toes. Are you happy now?"

Despite his grumbling and obvious embarrassment, he looked relaxed and comfortable with the men, Rachel thought. It was a revelation, seeing this side of him.

"Well, he got off to a rocky start," the fire boss went on, "but it didn't take him long before he was the best man on the crew. Wyatt here used to be one hell of a firefighter, ma'am. He could read a fire like it was a woman he'd just made love to. Always could figure out just the right moves, if you know what I mean."

Yes. I believe I know exactly what you mean. She made the mistake of glancing at Sam. He was watching her with that predatory glint in his eyes, and her insides quivered in remembered desire.

She hitched in a little breath, and it was as if they were alone on the mountainside. The clatter of dishes, the loud conversation around them, the other two men—everything else seemed to blur, leaving only the two of them wrapped up in the echoes of passion.

For an instant, she was back in his arms, reliving the incredible peace she found there, the lightning that skittered along her skin as those big, rough hands played over her, as that incredible mouth drew response after response from her.

As if he could read her mind, heat kindled in his eyes and she could see a muscle twitch in his cheek. He wanted her. She knew it as clearly as if he'd spoken the words aloud. If they hadn't been surrounded by people, he would have taken her, right there.

"Are you from Whiskey Creek?" she heard Charlie ask. "I can sure see why Wyatt won't leave that ranch of his, if you are."

Still flustered, her nerves scorching, Rachel scrambled to gather her thoughts to answer the fire boss. "No. I—I used to live here several years ago, but just came back to visit for a few weeks. I'm leaving tomorrow."

Sam stiffened beside her, and Rachel gave an inward groan. How did that slip out? She planned to tell him she was leaving, certainly, just not so abruptly.

"Rachel used to be my sister-in-law," he said, that strong, beautiful face suddenly expressionless, all trace of desire erased from it as if it had never been there at all. "She's Matt's widow."

Well, that put her in her place, she thought. Matt's

widow. That was all she was to him. Matt's widow, who had run out on her husband when he needed her. She slid her fork back onto the table, suddenly nauseous.

Immediately the two men's demeanor changed from slightly flirtatious to respectful, as if she were still dressed in black.

"I thought you looked familiar," Charlie said. "I must have seen you at his funeral. Matt was a great guy."

She laced her fingers together on her lap, unable to look at Sam. "Yes, he was."

Their jovial mood effectively shattered by the specter of her dead husband, the two other men quickly finished their meals and made their excuses.

Rachel managed to choke down a few more swallows of the soda, but couldn't bring herself to touch any of the food on her plate.

If she'd had the keys to the pickup, she would have packed up her shattered heart and driven out of here. Unfortunately, she knew even if she asked for them, Sam would refuse to hand them over. He'd made his feelings abundantly clear. Besides, he had to look out for Matt's spoiled, heedless little widow, didn't he?

She sighed, and it seemed to be the signal for Sam to gather their plates. Without speaking, he led the way to his tent, and she followed him, not knowing what else to do.

The sun had set in a blaze of glory and the pines shone black in the moonlight. The air had taken on a chill as well, and Rachel wished she'd had the foresight to bring along a jacket.

They walked in silence until he finally stopped several feet from his tent. "When were you going to tell me you were leaving?"

She glared at him, angry and hurting and unsure how to deal with any of it. "Right about the time you planned to tell me you were coming out on this fire."

"Dammit, Rachel. How do you think I felt hearing you say that so calmly. 'I'll be leaving tomorrow,' " he mimicked. "As if what we had together meant less than nothing to you."

"I imagine I thought you'd be relieved to have 'Matt's widow' out of your hair. You've practically been begging for me to leave since the day I stepped onto the Elkhorn."

"That was before," he growled.

"Before what?"

"Before we— Before I—" He clenched his hands into fists. "Dammit, just before."

She stared at him, then felt her anger fade, leaving only a devastating ache in her chest. She studied those strong features, his eyes that could glimmer with desire or blaze with determination or soften with affection toward his sons.

How could she be angry with him? It wasn't his fault he didn't return her love.

Dear heaven, how could she have been so stupid? In love with the one man who would never accept her, who might want her but who would never let himself see her as anything but the rich, spoiled woman who'd walked out on his best friend.

He ran a distracted hand through his hair. "I have to go back to work for a couple of hours. Try to get some rest. We can talk in the morning before you go."

She nodded, not trusting herself to say anything, and slipped inside his tent.

TWELVE

Rachel tried to punch the pillow into some semblance of comfort and finally rolled over in frustration. By all rights, she should be deep asleep by now. The day had been a long, exhausting, emotional one, and she felt wrung out, her energy store completely depleted.

All she could do was lie there, though, her mind whirring and her body filled with a restless need.

She turned her face into the pillow, wishing she could find some trace of Sam, that pine and leather smell of him. The pillowcase must have been newly washed, though, because all she could smell was the sweetness of laundry detergent.

She had taken one of his T-shirts out of the duffel at the foot of the tent to sleep in, but even those all smelled crisp and clean, with no trace of his scent. How pathetic was she, rooting around through his things like a piglet after truffles? Rachel groaned, then gave a ragged laugh at the image she must make.

She sighed and stared at the roof of the tent. She

couldn't handle this. Not again. She never thought she would have to go through it all again, this helpless need, these emotions that burned inside her with a physical, tangible hunger.

No, this was different, she corrected herself. What she'd felt for Matt had been strong. She couldn't deny that. He'd given her love and laughter at a time when she'd needed it desperately. But she couldn't cling to that for the rest of her life. Jo was right. She couldn't hide inside her pain and guilt forever. Sam had shown her she was ready to move on.

She had loved Matt. As she'd told Sam, part of her always would. But it had been a selfish, unhealthy kind of love. She could see that now. She'd wanted to keep him with her always, had been obsessively jealous of anything that took him away from her. Whenever he went out on a fire, she had been lost.

They had been teetering on shaky ground before she even left him, she acknowledged. She had been desperately unhappy in Whiskey Creek and Matt had simply refused to face that.

Maybe if he'd lived, if she'd had a little more time to grow up and into their marriage, they might have been able to forge a stronger union. Or maybe she would have ended up leaving him anyway, even without the added pressure of his firefighting.

She rolled over and punched the pillow again. Her feelings for Sam, while just as intense, seemed stronger, steadier. More centered. A woman's sure, firm love, instead of the obsessive devotion of a romantic girl.

Sam made her feel safe and warm. She always felt comforted when she was in his arms, she realized.

Though he was rough and ruggedly male, he had a deep streak of kindness in him. He was the kind of man strong enough to take on the world but gentle enough to make a woman feel nurtured, protected, cared for.

Why should she be so surprised she'd fallen in love with him? No. She gave a humorless laugh. It would have been more shocking if she could have spent two weeks with him and *not* fallen in love.

The snick of the tent flap zipper stirred her just as she slipped into the elusive arms of sleep. She lifted up onto her elbows to find him crouching in the door of the tent, backlit by the moon.

"You should be asleep," he said, his voice pitched low. "I'm sorry I woke you."

"You didn't. Not really. I was just dozing."

Bootless, he crept inside the tent and zipped the screen back up to keep the insects out. Immediately, the walls of the little canvas enclosure seemed to shrink around him. He filled the space, exuding energy and strength.

She sat up, awareness flooding through her in a hot tide. He looked beautiful there in the moonlight, and she yearned to reach for him, to pull that hard mouth to hers, to slip the T-shirt over her head and offer herself to him, to—

"I can bed down in the truck if you'd be more comfortable. Or out under the stars. I've done that plenty of times."

Rachel rapidly blinked away her thoughts, grateful for the concealing darkness that hid the blush she could feel spread from her shoulders to the roots of her hair.

"Is that . . . is that what you want? To sleep out under the stars?"

He swore softly. "You know it's not."

"Then don't. There's plenty of room right here. If you don't mind sharing, that is."

He was silent for a moment. "If I lie down on that sleeping bag with you, Rachel darlin', neither one of us is going to get any sleep."

The raw need in his voice sent another tremor rippling through her, and she smiled in the dark. "Yes. I know."

He groaned and reached for her. He must have unbuttoned his shirt before he opened the tent flap, because she could feel the heated sleekness of his skin under her fingers.

His scent overwhelmed her, and she inhaled deeply, trying to burn the moment into her memory. This was what she'd been looking for when she'd pawed through his things. This connection. If she'd ever needed the comfort she found with him, tonight was the night.

"I haven't been able to think about anything but this since I saw you leaning over the bed of Jo's truck earlier tonight," he murmured. "No, that's not true. I've been making love to you in my mind since two weeks ago when you showed up at my ranch with your fancy car and those legs that go on forever."

She made her voice prim, while inside she brimmed, overflowed, with sensual awareness. "Why, Sam Wyatt. You dirty old man."

"Damn straight," he said, and reached for her again.

More than anything, she would miss this. The

laughter and exhilaration and wonder she found with
him. An ache spread through her that had nothing to
do with desire and everything to do with heartbreak.
This was her last chance to be with him, to bask in the
heat of his arms.

Despair edging her motions, she kissed him ar-
dently. She couldn't get close enough to him, couldn't
touch him enough. She slipped her arms around him
inside his shirt, relishing the hardness of his muscle,
the solid strength that engulfed her.

Unprepared for the fierceness of her embrace, he
lost his balance and toppled backward onto the blanket,
pulling her with him.

She could feel his chuckle vibrating against her.
"Whoa, darlin'. Slow down. We've got all night."

That's all we've got. Tonight, she almost said, but decided not to waste her energy with words. Futile, useless words. Instead she rose to a sitting position and
straddled him, her knees on either side of his hips, then
lifted the T-shirt over her head.

In the dim light inside the tent, she couldn't see his
expression, but he became completely still, the only
sound his ragged breathing.

"You're so beautiful," he said, his voice hoarse,
gravelly. "I wish I could come up with the right words.
That I could figure out how to tell you what you do to
me."

"Don't tell me," she whispered. "Just show me."

He slid one rough hand to her face, to her cheek,
and the tender intimacy of his touch nearly destroyed
her. She leaned into his hand, eyes closed, her heart
pulsing loudly in her ears.

For a long time they remained motionless, and then slowly—agonizingly slowly—he glided his hand down her throat, down her chest, to one swollen breast.

"If I had to describe your skin," he said, still in that hoarse whisper, "I'd say it's softer than the most finely polished wood. Not very romantic, I know, but that's what it feels like to me."

He paused. "I love your eyes when they turn all smoky. They make me think of the sky above the Elkhorn during an August thunderstorm, full of passion and energy. And when you've got your hair down like this instead of in those ponytail things you usually wear around the ranch, it's all I can do not to go to you and bury my hands in it, to burn my fingers in all that fire."

With each word, her bones, her muscles, seemed to dissolve into him. Her senses were heightened, and she felt as if she could feel every single nerve impulse firing inside her skin.

She closed her eyes, trying to catch her breath, and he pulled her close to him, his mouth buried in her hair.

"Every time I see you, you become more beautiful to me. Not just here." He ran his hand along her cheek again, then down to the valley between her breasts, where her heart beat thinly, rapidly. "But here. Especially here, Rachel."

He worshiped her with his mouth, with his hands, with his body, and when the heat faded and he held her in his arms for what she knew would be the last time, Rachel thought she could hear her heart ripping apart.

Gradually she fell asleep, her head cradled in the crook of his shoulder, and Sam stroked her hair absently, his gaze fastened on the canvas of the tent. He could see a tiny hole near the seam where a little pinprick of moonlight showed through.

He'd have to get that repaired before Zach used it on his next Scout campout, he thought. Wouldn't do to have the boy out in the middle of a rainstorm in a leaky tent. Then again, maybe it was time to buy each of the boys a tent of their own. They were getting old enough they'd both be going on campouts soon.

He sighed. *Nice try, Wyatt. Distract yourself so you don't have to think about the morning.*

The morning. When Rachel would be leaving, taking her sunshine and her sweetness out of his life. The very idea of it filled him with something close to anguish.

He was in love with her, he realized. All this time, he thought it had only been desire, but he'd been fooling himself. He loved the woman who gave herself so freely to him. Who made him laugh with her smart mouth that hid a soft vulnerability. Who loved his sons like they were her own.

She *should* have children of her own. For an instant, he had a vivid image of her swollen with a child—with his child—and clenched his fists as a fierce longing stabbed through him.

His movement must have awakened her because she stirred sleepily. "What time is it?"

He shrugged, pushing away his thoughts. "About two, I'd guess."

"You're going to be one tired cowboy in the morning."

"I'll live," he said, then added honestly, "I wanted to hold you while I still could."

"Oh, Sam." She hesitated, as if picking her words carefully. "You know, I could stay. For a little while longer, anyway."

For an instant, he was tempted. Maybe he could convince her to stay forever if he had more time. Then reality reared its ugly head. He didn't have anything to offer her but a used-up old ranch, a struggling construction company, and a couple of half-grown kids.

"What would be the use?" he mumbled. "It'd just be putting off the inevitable."

She opened her mouth as if to argue, but he cut her off. "I've been thinking, though. You were right. The boys need a little taste of life outside Whiskey Creek. If you still want them to come at Christmas, I don't see the harm in it."

He thought she would have been thrilled by the idea. He didn't really want the boys to go, but he knew it would make her happy. Instead, when she spoke, her voice was subdued, as if all the life had been sucked away.

"Thank you. I'll make the arrangements and let you know about them. I'll pay for their flights, of course."

He bristled. "I can afford it. I might not have your daddy's kind of money, but I'm not doin' so bad."

She didn't argue, just nodded her head and slid away from him. Immediately, he missed her closeness and wanted to pull her back to him, but she was slipping her arms through the sleeves of his T-shirt, covering up all that glorious skin.

"I'm sorry. I never meant to imply that you

weren't," she said quietly, still in that empty voice he hated.

Anger snapped to life. He was doing this for her. Why was she suddenly acting like he'd just kicked her dog or something?

"I thought you wanted them to come out for a visit. If you don't, just say so."

"This has nothing to do with the boys," she said, her tone suddenly bristling with as much anger as his. "It's about you and me, Sam, and you know it."

"I don't know anything anymore. I just know I hate the idea of you leaving."

"Then ask me to stay. I'd do it in a heartbeat."

"Stay." The word escaped before he could swallow it.

She froze. "Do you mean it?"

"I said it, didn't I?" he grumbled.

She laughed, lilting sweetness inside the canvas walls of the tent. "Now say it like you mean it."

All the arguments running through his head about how she didn't belong faded away when compared to the pain he felt at her leaving. The only thing left was the one compelling reason why she should stay—that he loved her and didn't want to see her drive out of his life. Nothing else was important.

"Stay, Rachel. For a week or two weeks or however long you can afford to be away from work."

"Yes."

He continued as if he hadn't heard her. "I don't know where we're going with this, but I think we owe it to ourselves to see. I . . . care about you. More than I ever thought I could care about a woman again."

She smiled. "You have a very sweet way with words when you want to, Sam Wyatt," she whispered, then touched her mouth to his.

He pulled her against him and held her for a long time, until he could feel his body stir to life again, then he slowly slid his hand inside the T-shirt to caress the bare skin of her back.

"Wyatt? You asleep?"

He growled against her mouth at the voice from outside the tent, and Rachel laughed softly.

"Yeah, I'm asleep," he said. "Go away, Charlie."

"Can't. I need to talk to you. We've got one hell of a problem."

Rachel suddenly became aware that the noise level in the fire camp had picked up. It was still much quieter than it had been before dark, but she could hear shouting in the distance, muffled conversations, the hum of motors.

Sam must have sensed it, too, because he immediately reached for his jeans and slid them on before opening the tent flap. The fire boss was crouched outside, looking even more exhausted in the moonlight than he had earlier in the evening.

Through the thin walls of the tent, she could hear their conversations as clearly as if she'd been standing beside them.

"What's up?" Sam asked immediately.

"The fire jumped a line on the south edge and is heading for a couple of ranches down there."

"The Rocking L and Widow Peterson's place. Damn. I thought that area was secured."

"Yeah, so did we. It hasn't spread too far, at this

point, but if we don't contain it soon, those places will be destroyed."

"So send a crew down there to clean it up and keep it from going farther."

"I don't have a crew to send." Rachel could clearly hear frustration edging the fire boss's voice. "Some of these guys have been out for twenty-plus hours right now, Sam. It's just not safe to send them out again."

"Call in reinforcements, then. How hard can that be?"

"Why do you think I've been on the damn phone for the last hour? I've rattled every cage I can at the Interagency Fire Center, but the earliest they can get anybody fresh out here is noon tomorrow. By then I'm afraid it will be too late."

"Why are you telling me all this?"

The fire boss paused, and Rachel held her breath, knowing what was coming next.

"I need you, Wyatt. I only have one crew that's not flat-out exhausted. The mop-up crew. The greenest of the green. I need somebody with experience to lead them out there."

"No." Sam bit out the word. "Absolutely not."

"Sam—"

"How many damn times do we have to have this conversation, Charlie? I haven't been out in the field for five years. I'd be worse than the most raw recruit you've got out there."

"Bull. You know exactly what you need to do. You just don't want to do it."

"Exactly. I don't want to, and last time I checked, this was still a free country."

"You turn me down, Sam, and you'll be to blame if anything goes wrong out there. Are you willing to deal with that?"

They must have walked away. Although Rachel strained her ears as hard as she could, she couldn't hear Sam's answer.

She waited in the tent for him to return, feeling numb, as if she'd been immersed in icy water.

Just when she was about to go racing after them to give Sam all the reasons why he couldn't go out on the fire, why she wouldn't let him, a rustle near the tent door signaled his return.

She didn't need to see the expression on his face to know Charlie had won the argument. It was stamped in the determined set of his shoulders, in the stubborn angle of his chin.

Her bubbling joy of a few minutes before, when he'd asked her to stay at the ranch, dissipated like a bottle of champagne left uncorked.

"You're going, then?" Her voice sounded as rough as forty-grit sandpaper.

"I have to, Rachel."

"You don't *have* to. Somebody else could do it."

"Not this time. Lord knows, putting Nomex on again is the last thing I want to do, but there's nobody else."

She fiercely tried to tamp down the fear rushing through her, the bitter taste of terror that nearly choked her. The past and the present and the future all seemed to merge into one undulating, red-orange nightmare. She took a shaky breath as flames chased each other through her mind, as she remembered the crushing shock of Sam knocking on the door of that awful motel room five years ago.

She had known then, even before he spoke, what he would say. She had known, somehow, Matt was gone. She had survived it once, but she knew she wouldn't be able to survive it again.

She wouldn't beg, though. Pain-filled memories washed through her of that last fire Matt had gone on. She had begged then, had pleaded with him until her throat was raw.

Don't go. Not on this one.

They had fought most of the night about it, and when her entreaties hadn't worked, she'd turned to threats. *I can't live like this, Matt. If you choose the fire, I won't be here when you get back.*

In the end, she lost the bitter competition. The irresistible lure of the flames had won again. Matt had loved her and still he had chosen the fire. She knew she stood no chance of convincing Sam not to go.

Through the haze in her mind, she realized he'd slid on his boots and was grabbing another T-shirt out of the duffel and tugging it down over his chest.

"I don't know what time I'll be back, but Charlie seems to think the replacements will be here by morning. Wait for me, Rachel, and I'll drive you back to the Elkhorn as soon as I can, all right?"

She didn't trust herself to answer him, so she merely nodded, although she had no intention of sitting there patiently waiting for him. Not again. Never again.

With one quick, distracted kiss, he was gone.

THIRTEEN

The sun was high overhead by the time Rachel drove her little rental car along the dusty dirt road away from the Elkhorn.

The boys and Josie stood on the porch watching her, and Noah still had a red nose and tears trickling down his face, even though she'd spent the last half hour consoling him after she'd told him she was leaving. It had helped a little to tell him his father had said both boys could come to visit her at Christmas, but he was still distraught she was leaving.

Her eyes felt grainy from lack of sleep and from the effort she'd made all morning to keep her emotions in check. Rachel wanted nothing more than to lean her head against the steering wheel and have a good cry herself, but she knew that wasn't the answer. She would have plenty of time to fall apart when she returned to California. Right now, she needed to put as much distance as possible between her and Whiskey Creek, Wyoming.

With effort, she managed to set her mind on auto-pilot for the hour-long trip to Jackson, focusing only on the motions involved in driving. If she didn't, she knew she would completely surrender to the heartache of leaving it all behind.

Sam would be angry, she knew, that she'd left so abruptly. Throughout the morning, she'd forced herself not to think about it. She'd waited until the first pearly light of dawn, lying stiff and awake for hours on the sleeping bag where they'd made love, before taking her keys from the pocket of the work shirt he'd been wearing earlier.

The drive away from the fire camp had been as emotionally draining as her trip the day before. Instead of nerves, though, she'd been filled with pain and loss. Consumed by it as surely as the fire was devouring everything in its path.

She reached the outskirts of Jackson several hours before her flight was scheduled to leave. The time stretched out ahead of her, stark and empty. The idea of sitting and waiting in the little airport held no appeal to her, so she decided to spend the remaining hours wandering through the shops of the tourist town. It would give her a good chance to find a gift for her father and something to repay Anna, her assistant at the foundation, for filling in so long in her absence.

After she located a parking slot near the town square, Rachel slid out of the convertible and into the muggy air. The heat seemed worse here amid the pavement and buildings, churned up by traffic and people. It settled on everything, sucking away whatever energy she had left.

Despite the heat, she could see storm clouds gathering to the east. Maybe the long drought was finally about to break. She just prayed it would be a nice gentle summer rain with plenty of precipitation instead of a violent thunderstorm. The last thing the crews fighting the chain of fires in the region needed was an electrical storm, where lightning would inevitably kindle more blazes in the dry growth.

She jerked her mind away from fires, from Sam, and forced herself to walk through the brightly painted door of a gift shop. Her heart just wasn't in it, though. She couldn't drum up enthusiasm for anything there, so she continued looking through several other stores along the main square, then wandered down a side street.

She walked listlessly out of the fourth art gallery without finding anything she thought would appeal either to her father or to Anna. Looking around, she happened to glance across the street. Instantly, she froze.

How could she have forgotten it? The little motel where she'd waited in vain for Matt was just across the street, looking as disreputable as ever: squat and plain, with the paint still peeling, the neon still burned out in several letters of its name.

For an instant it was as if she'd crossed back through the years. All her feelings of that day, that terrible day she'd found out about Matt's death, came rushing back.

Compelled by a need she couldn't name, Rachel crossed the street, barely even noticing the driver of a recreational vehicle who slammed on the brakes and honked long and angrily at her.

She reached the sidewalk on the other side of the street and stood staring at the building, awash in the past.

Sam had been so kind that night, she remembered. She'd forgotten that in the trauma of the days that followed. That memory had been supplanted by the one of their confrontation after the funeral, when she had told him she was leaving and he had reacted with anger and disdain.

That had been later. The night he had come for her at the motel, he had quietly told her Matt had died, then had gathered her into his strong arms and held her. She hadn't cried. Hadn't even reacted at all, she remembered. She'd just stood there in his arms, feeling as if all her emotions, every last living cell inside her, had crumbled away into nothing.

He'd gathered her things for her, she remembered with a poignant ache. She hadn't really unpacked anything, she had been so certain Matt would come for her soon, but Sam had silently collected the nightgown she'd slept in, her few toiletries, the paperback she'd been pretending to read all day, then had led her to his truck to take her home.

She clasped a fist to her mouth. Home. The Elkhorn was home to her, whether she wanted to admit it or not. Her father's house had been just a place to live, the empty husk that sheltered her from rain and wind. But the Elkhorn had been home, even then.

She had found love there, not once but twice. And she had thrown it away.

Not once, but twice.

Rachel closed her eyes and her chin sagged onto her chest. Oh, Lord, what had she done? She'd walked away *again* from the only thing that mattered to her. From Sam. From Jo. From the boys, whom she loved as deeply as if they'd come from her own womb. All because she had been too afraid, too selfish to let someone she loved make his own decisions.

Sam hadn't gone out on the fire to hurt her, any more than Matt had. He went because that's who he was—the kind of man who looked out for the people he cared about, who simply had to take action when it was within his power.

He'd helped Jo by buying back the Elkhorn ranchland she'd been forced to sell. He'd protected Matt when they'd fought fires together. She had no doubt he'd watched out for his father all those years they'd been on the move.

He'd even taken care of her the day he had come for her, when he had held her so tenderly at this damn motel.

Why should it surprise her when he put his life on the line to protect his neighbors, the community that had taken him in? No, he hadn't done it to hurt her. He had done it because he didn't have a choice. If he *had* been able to walk away, he wouldn't be the man she'd fallen in love with.

A fierce determination settled on her shoulders. She wasn't leaving. She couldn't. Even if he sent her away, she would just keep coming back, again and again, until she wore down his resistance. She loved Sam Wyatt with everything she had in her, and she was going to stick to him like a burr on a blanket until he was willing to accept that.

He loved her too. She knew it as surely as she knew the seasons would soon change in Whiskey Creek. She remembered the tenderness in his gaze last night. *"I wanted to hold you while I still had the chance,"* he had said.

She wasn't running away from that. Not this time. Her heart fluttering like a thousand butterflies caught in a silken net, she rushed back to her rental car.

Sam was probably still at the fire camp. She would stop at the Elkhorn long enough to borrow Josie's pickup for the mountainous trip, she decided, then drive there to meet him.

The sky seemed to darken more with each mile she traveled back to the ranch. Back home. By the time she drove under the log arch at the entrance, the clouds were so gray they were nearly black, fat with what she hoped was healing, blessed moisture.

See? she thought. She was even thinking like a rancher. She laughed a little, her heart pumping hard in her chest with nerves and adrenaline, and pulled to a stop in front of the ranch house in a flurry of dust and gravel.

The boys were nowhere in sight, but just as Rachel climbed out of the rental car Josie walked out onto the wide porch, wiping her hands on her apron.

A wide, knowing grin split her angular face. "I've been watchin' for you. Figured you'd be back before nightfall."

Rachel stared. "What do you mean? Why would you possibly think I'd be back?"

"Women's intuition." Josie cackled. " 'Sides that, you're a smart gal. I knew it likely wouldn't take you long to come to your senses."

"If I were smart, Jo, I never would have left in the first place." She managed a shaky smile. "Anyway, would you mind if I borrowed your pickup again?"

"What the heck for?"

"I need to go back to the fire camp. To find Sam."

"Well, you can borrow it, but I'm afraid you won't find Sam at any fire camp. He came back an hour ago. I guess a bunch of fresh firefighters came in this morning, so that fire boss fellow sent him home."

"Is he . . . is he all right?"

Josie shrugged. "Seemed to be. Tired and kinda distant, but he seemed fine to me. The boys are down showin' him that treehouse you all have been workin' on so hard."

Now that she was there, how did she tell him she was staying? What had seemed so easy on the drive back was now as insurmountable as those mountains in the background. What if he didn't want her? What if she'd misinterpreted everything?

Some of her turmoil must have shown on her face, because Jo shook her head, reached out, and pulled Rachel into a tight hug. "Now, don't you go chickenin' out on me. You did the right thing, comin' back."

With a tremulous smile, she hugged the older woman, then pulled away. "Thanks, Josie. Let's just hope Sam feels the same way."

❖━━━━━━❖

The ramshackle treehouse looked like it would topple in the first good wind, and Sam wondered if he had the fortitude to let the boys climb up on the thing.

They'd picked a sturdy maple tree to build it in, he'd say that much for his sons, one with branches that spread thick and wide. But the treehouse itself was constructed of uneven, mismatched scrap wood and it dipped dangerously to one side.

Maybe he could find some way to reinforce it without hurting their feelings. No, he could let it go for now, he decided. Deal with it another day. He didn't want to say anything that might dampen what little enthusiasm they were displaying, especially since both of them were trying so hard not to show him how much Rachel's leaving had devastated them.

"Looks like you boys have the makings of two fine carpenters. Another couple of years and I might just have to put you both on my crew."

"Aunt Rachel did a lot of the work," Zach said loyally. "She's the one who had the idea of the window so we could watch to see who was comin'. You know, Dad, she's a pretty good carpenter too."

"And a real good cook," Noah put in, giving his father a pointed look. "I didn't even mind Brussels sprouts when she fixed 'em. Well, not too much, anyways."

Despite his exhaustion and the fierce pain lodged firmly in his chest, Sam nearly laughed at their transparent matchmaking attempts. Bad enough that Josie had apparently thrust her meddling nose in where it didn't belong. It appeared he would have to put up with the same thing from his sons.

He sighed. "Boys, Aunt Rachel's gone. I know it hurts, but that's the way it is. We were real lucky that she could stay with us as long as she could, but she had a life she had to get back to."

"Yeah, but she didn't want to leave," Noah said. "I just know it. When she hugged us good-bye she had tears in her eyes." Noah looked like he was on the verge of tears again himself, and Sam gave a mental groan.

"If you asked her, I know she'd come back," Zach added.

How long was he going to have to cope with this? He was so tired, he just wanted to crawl into his bed and not climb out for days. He didn't know if he had the strength left to handle his boys' emotional trauma, to calmly give them all the reasons why Rachel didn't belong there, why she had to leave.

Not when he was having a hard enough time convincing himself, anyway.

He had to admit, he hadn't really been surprised when he arrived back at the fire camp to find her gone. He had known, somehow. Had felt a hollowness in his gut even before he walked back to his silent, empty tent that still smelled of her.

He even understood it. His decision to go out on the fire must have been a bitter repeat of her life with Matt. He should have realized she would have a tough time handling it.

Maybe subconsciously that was even why he decided to go out on the fire, to show her how wrong they were for each other. *The truth hurts, doesn't it?* He grimaced. Whether he wanted to admit it or not, he was still running from the feelings she sparked in him.

No, he hadn't been surprised when she left. But he wondered if this pain would ever go away.

Sighing again, he turned to find the boys watching him with the same hopeful look on each of their faces, as if he could magically kiss this hurt away like he did with skinned knees and bruised elbows.

Aw, hell. What was he supposed to do now? He crouched down to their level and pulled them to him, one boy in each arm. "Guys, we're all going to miss her. It hurts a lot when somebody you love goes away. But we just have to go on."

Yeah, good advice. So why did it suddenly seem impossible for him to follow?

"Besides," he went on, "it's not like we won't ever see her again. And you can still talk to her on the phone and write her letters, can't you?"

Was any of this registering with them? Zach looked like he was listening, but Noah didn't even seem to be paying attention. He was peering off over Sam's shoulder, toward the house, an intent look on his freckled face.

If the boy could conjure up Rachel just by concentration alone, Sam thought, he had no doubt she would have been walking down the path.

"I'm sorry, Noah. I know you'll miss her, but you're going to see Aunt Rachel at Christmas. That's only a few more mo—"

Noah suddenly shouted and pulled away from Sam's arms before he could finish his sentence. "She's back! I knew it! I knew she'd come back!"

"Son—"

Noah didn't listen, just tore off toward the house. Frowning, Sam stood and turned, expecting to see Josie walking toward him and wondering how he would console Noah after one more in a long, hard day of disappointments.

Instead when he turned, all he could do was stare at the sight of Rachel standing two hundred feet away, her arms outstretched to catch his son barreling toward her.

"Noah's right! It *is* Aunt Rachel!" Zach pulled away from him, too, and took off, leaving Sam standing alone.

She hugged them both tightly and rocked them in her arms for a long time before letting them go. They were too far away for him to hear what she said to them, but she gestured back toward the house. Though both boys shook their heads, she must have prevailed, because they hugged her once more then raced together in the direction of the house.

She watched them go, then turned back to him. Even from this distance he could see nervousness flit across her face, and she clasped her hands together as she began walking toward him.

Confusion and amazement and a vast joy at seeing her again—a joy he knew damn well he shouldn't be feeling—swept through him, and he started along the fence line to meet her.

A dozen questions jumbled through his mind, but when he reached her he asked the first one that came to him. "What did you say to the boys to send them rushing back to the house like that?"

She watched him carefully out of those gray doe eyes. "Just that I needed to speak with you alone for a few minutes. They seemed to understand."

Good thing at least somebody understood what was going on, because he sure didn't. He had resigned himself to the fact that she was gone, and here she was standing in front of him, looking as sweetly beautiful as ever.

"What are you doing back? Did you forget something?"

Her mouth twisted into a tiny smile before straightening out again. "In a manner of speaking, yes."

He frowned. "What does that mean?"

"Aren't you even going to say hello?"

"Hello. What are you doing here, Rachel? Jo said your plane was supposed to leave Jackson at five-thirty."

"That's right."

He gave a raw-sounding laugh. "I'm afraid you're going to miss it. It's nearly that now."

"Yes, I know."

"So what are you doing here?"

"Just like you said. I forgot something. Something I discovered I couldn't live without."

"What's that?"

She smiled at him then, a stunning, pure smile that took his breath away. "The people I love. They're all right here."

"Rachel—"

Was he happy to see her? She couldn't tell. Those beautiful blue eyes were shuttered, his expression stony. She could swear she'd seen relief in his eyes when he'd first seen her, but now she could read nothing there.

She wiped suddenly moist hands on her slacks. "I couldn't leave, Sam. I tried, but I—I realized I didn't have anything waiting for me in Santa Barbara. Nothing but a cold, empty existence. Here I have so much, all the people I love. Jo and the boys. And you," she added quietly. "Especially you."

He closed his eyes for a moment, as if her words hurt him. When he opened them, they burned with tangled emotions: pain and longing and regret.

"You have a life there," he said. "A job you love. I can't ask you to stay, Rachel. I can't. It wouldn't be fair to you."

"You already did, last night at the fire camp. Remember? I'm not going to let you go back on your word now, Sam Wyatt. Besides, all I need is a telephone, a computer, and a fax machine, and I easily can run the foundation from here."

Her carefully thought-out solution just seemed to anger him. "Why can't you get it through your head? You don't belong here. You're furs and fancy hors d'oeuvres. I'm flannel shirts and burgers on the grill."

She winced as he shouted the last words to her, but she refused to back down, not when their future was at stake. "I love burgers on the grill," she said, fighting to keep her voice calm. "And flannel shirts too."

"Dammit, Rachel, will you listen to me?"

"No, I won't. Not if you're going to go over this again. How many times do I have to prove myself to you? I've changed. I'm not that stupid, selfish girl anymore and you know it. I don't need furs or fancy hors d'oeuvres. I never have."

She paused, longing to reach out to him but not daring. Not yet. "I need love, Sam, and I've found that here. I've loved every minute of the last two weeks, of being here with you. I've been happy, really happy for the first time in my life."

Sam thought of her working on the treehouse with the boys, of them riding across the meadow together, of her gentle care with Jo. She was different, he couldn't deny that. Was it enough, though?

He wanted her to stay more than he remembered wanting anything in his life, but how could he risk it? There was more at stake than his own heart. It would destroy the boys if they thought she was coming back to stay and she ended up changing her mind and returning to California.

"What about today?" he asked. "About the fire? What if I decide I want to go back to that life?"

She faced him, her chin lifted. "Then I'll be waiting and worrying about you until you come home. But I won't try to stop you and I *will* be here, every single time you come back."

He gripped the fence railing so tightly his knuckles turned white. "Didn't you learn anything with Matt?"

"Yes," she said. "I learned a great deal. Especially how to love someone deeply. Because I did it once, it was that much easier to recognize when it happened again. I love you, Sam Wyatt. Whether you like it or not, I love you."

Rachel held her breath, praying he wouldn't turn away. She didn't know if she could bear it.

The seconds stretched between them, long and painful, and then, just as she felt the first plop of rain on her face and thought he would reject her, he muttered an oath and reached for her. A sigh of relief escaped her as he slid his arms around her and pulled her against his chest, her cheek nestled to his heart.

"I hope to hell you mean it, Rachel, because I'm not letting you go again. I swear I'm not. You're staying put this time, if I have to nail your shoes to the floor."

Like spring coming to the mountains after a long, cold winter, joy blossomed through her. "Where would I go? Everything I need is right here."

She was laughing and crying at the same time when he dipped his head to kiss her, and the rain fell in earnest, soaking into the thirsty ground in huge drops. She didn't care when it drenched her hair, her clothes, when it trickled down her back. The only thing that mattered was Sam, the strength of his arms around her, the fierceness of his kiss.

She was home.

They stood there for a long time, bodies and souls entwined, and finally he pulled away. He studied her for a moment, then tenderly drew his hard, callused thumb across her wet cheek. "I love you, Rachel Lawrence."

She closed her eyes, letting the sweetness of it wash through her, but he didn't give her time to savor the words she'd waited so long to hear.

"I meant what I said," he told her. "I'm not letting you go. Argue all you want, but you're going to marry me."

She opened her eyes and gave him a pointed look. "Are you asking me or telling me?"

He grinned. "Both, I guess."

The laughter quickly faded from his expression, and he reached for her hands. "It's not an easy life, Rachel. You know that. There's no mercy in a land like this. The winters are long and cruel and the work is hard, constant."

"I know. And the summers can be worse, especially in a bad fire season. I understand all that, that I might not see you for weeks at a time. It's all right, Sam. As long as you come home to me, that's all that matters."

He shook his head. "I'm not going out on any more fires. Today just convinced me I don't need that anymore. The whole time I was out there, all I could think about was being with you."

"Oh, Sam." Tears filled her eyes, and he drew her back into his kiss.

After several long, wonderful moments, he lifted his head. "Is that a yes?"

"What was the question again?" she teased.

"Will you stay? Marry me and run your father's foundation from here and be a mother to my boys? And maybe give me a couple of beautiful red-haired babies on down the line?"

"I don't have red hair," she huffed, but she could feel the tears well up in her eyes again at the very idea of those babies.

He grinned. "Let me rephrase that. Give me a couple of beautiful, uh, auburn-haired babies?"

"Dark-haired babies," she insisted. "Like their daddy."

"I can live with that. What do you say?"

Their gazes locked, and she smiled at the love she could see brimming out of those deep, endlessly blue eyes. "Yes, Sam. A million times, yes."

He grinned. "Why don't we go make two boys delirious with joy and tell them you're staying?"

She laughed, imagining their reaction. "I don't know who's going to be happier, Jo or the boys."

He rubbed his thumb across the curve of her cheekbone. "Me. I'm going to be the happiest. Don't you ever forget that, Rachel."

Their hands linked, they turned and walked through the healing rain toward the house. Toward the future.

THE EDITORS' CORNER

The new year is once again upon us, and we're ushering it in with four new LOVESWEPTs to grace your bookshelves. From the mountains of Kentucky and Nevada to the beaches of Florida, we'll take you to places only your heart can go! So curl up in a comfy chair and hide out from the rest of the world while you plan a christening party with Peggy, catch a killer with Ruth, rescue a pirate with Cynthia, and camp out in the Sierras with Jill.

First is **ANGELS ON ZEBRAS**, LOVESWEPT #866, by the well-loved Peggy Webb. Attorney Joseph Patrick Beauregard refuses to allow Maxie Corban to include zebras at their godson's christening party. Inappropriate, he says. And that's just the beginning! Joe likes his orderly life just fine, and Maxie can't help but try to shake it up by playing the brazen hussy to Joe's conservative legal eagle. Suffice it to say, a steamy yet tenuous relationship ensues, as they learn they can't keep their hands off each other! You may remember Joe and Maxie's relatives as B. J. Corban and Crash Beauregard from BRINGING UP BAXTER, LOVESWEPT #847. Peggy Webb stuns us with another sensual tale of love and laughter in this enchanting mix of sizzle and whimsy.

Ex-cop Rafe Ramirez has no choice but to become the hero of a little girl determined to save her mom in Ruth Owen's **SOMEONE TO WATCH OVER ME,** LOVESWEPT #867. TV anchorwoman Tory Chandler has been receiving dangerous riddles and rhymes written in bloodred ink. Knowing her past is about to rear its ugly head, she wants nothing more than to ignore the threats that have her on edge. Rafe can't ignore them, however, since he's given Tory's daughter his word. Protecting the beautiful temptress who so openly betrayed him is the hardest assignment he's ever had to face. Now that he's back on the road to recovery, can this compassionate warrior keep Tory safe from her worst nightmares? LOVESWEPT favorite Ruth Owen explores the healing of two wounded souls in this story of dark emotions and desperate yearnings.

In **YOUR PLACE OR MINE?,** LOVESWEPT #868, by Cynthia Powell, Captain Diego Swift wakes to find himself stranded in a time much different from his own, and becomes engaged in an argument with the demure she-devil who has besieged his home. Catalina Steadwell had prayed for help from above, though admittedly this half-drowned, naked sailor was not what she was expecting. Though Cat doesn't believe this man's ravings about the nineteenth century, she does need a man around her dilapidated house, and hires Diego as her handyman. After all, the job market for pirates has pretty much dwindled to nothing. When Diego becomes involved in a local gang war, he learns to make use of his second chance at life and love. Here's a positively scrumptious tale by Cynthia Powell that's sure to fulfill every woman's dream of a seafaring, swashbuckling hero!

In **SHOW ME THE WAY,** LOVESWEPT #869, by Jill Shalvis, Katherine Wilson ventures into the wilds of the high Sierras in a desperate attempt to stay alive. Outfitter Kyle Spencer challenges the pretty prosecutor to accompany his group in conquering the elements, but Katy is a city girl at heart. As danger stalks them through God's country, suddenly nothing in the woods is as innocent as it seems. Kyle knows that something is terrifying Katy and wants desperately to help her, but how can he when the woman won't let him near her? Their attraction grows as their time together ebbs, and soon Katy will have to make a choice. Will she entrust Kyle with her life and her heart, or will the maniac who's after her succeed in destroying her? In this journey of survival and discovery, Jill Shalvis shows us once again how believing in love can save you from yourself.

Happy reading!

With warmest wishes,

Susann Brailey

Joy Abella

Susann Brailey   Joy Abella

Senior Editor   Administrative Editor

P.S. Look for these Bantam women's fiction titles coming in January! National bestseller Patricia Potter delivers **STARCATCHER.** On the eve before Lady Marsali Mackey's wedding, she is kidnapped by Patrick Sutherland, Earl of Trydan, and the man who had promised to marry her twelve years ago. And Lisa Gardner, who may be familiar as Silhouette author Alicia Scott, makes her chilling suspense debut with **THE PERFECT HUSBAND,** a novel about a woman who teams up with a mercenary to catch a serial killer. And immediately following this page, preview the Bantam women's fiction titles on sale in November!

For current information on Bantam's women's fiction, visit our new Web site, *Isn't It Romantic,* at the following address:
                http://www.bdd.com/romance

Don't miss these extraordinary books
from your favorite Bantam authors!

On sale in November:

TIDINGS OF GREAT JOY
by Sandra Brown

LONG AFTER MIDNIGHT
by Iris Johansen

TABOO
by Susan Johnson

STOLEN MOMENTS
by Michelle Martin

Get swept away by the classic Christmas romance
from *New York Times* bestselling author

Sandra Brown

TIDINGS OF GREAT JOY

Available in hardcover!

*Ria Lavender hadn't planned on spending a passionate
Christmas night in front of a roaring fire with Taylor
MacKensie. But somehow the scents of pine tree, wood
smoke, and male flesh produced a kind of spontaneous com-
bustion inside her, and morning found the lonely architect
lying on her silver fox coat beside the mayor-elect, a man
she hardly knew. Ten weeks later she was pregnant with
Taylor's child . . . and insisted they had to marry. A
marriage "in name only," she promised him, to protect the
innocent baby, with an annulment right after the birth.
Taylor agreed to the wedding, but shocked Ria with his
demand that they live together as husband and wife—in
every way. She couldn't deny she wanted him, the lady-
killer with the devil's grin, but there was danger in suc-
cumbing to the heat he roused—in falling for a man she
couldn't keep. Taylor knew the child she carried bound her
to him, but could his rough and tender loving be the miracle gift she longed for?*

Now in paperback!

LONG AFTER MIDNIGHT

by *New York Times* bestselling author

Iris Johansen

The first warning was triggered hundreds of miles away. The second warning exploded only yards from where she and her son stood. Now Kate Denby realizes the frightening truth: She is somebody's target.

Danger has arrived in Kate's backyard with a vengeance. And the gifted scientist is awakening to a nightmare world where a ruthless killer is stalking her . . . where her innocent son is considered expendable . . . and where the medical research to which she has devoted her life is the same research that could get her killed. Her only hope of protecting her family and making that medical breakthrough is to elude her enemy until she can face him on her own ground, on her own terms—and destroy him.

Joshua remained awake for almost an hour, and even after his eyes finally closed, he slept fitfully.

It was just as well they were going away, Kate thought. Joshua wasn't a high-strung child, but what he'd gone through was enough to unsettle anyone.

Phyliss's door was closed, Kate noted when she reached the hall. She should probably get to bed too. Not that she'd be able to sleep. She hadn't lied to Joshua; she was nervous and uneasy . . . and bitterly resentful. This was her home, it was supposed to be a haven. She didn't like to think of it as a fortress.

But, like it or not, it was a fortress at the moment and she'd better make sure the soldiers were on the battlements. She checked the lock on the front door before she moved quickly toward the living room. She would see the black-and-white from the picture window.

Phyliss, as usual, had drawn the drapes over the window before she went to bed. The cave instinct, Kate thought as she reached for the cord. Close out the outside world and make your own. She and Phyliss were in complete agree—

He was standing outside the window, so close they were separated only by a quarter of an inch of glass.

Oh God. High concave cheekbones, long black straight hair drawn back in a queue, beaded necklace. It was him . . . Ishmaru.

And he was smiling at her.

His lips moved and he was so near she could hear the words through the glass. "You weren't supposed to see me before I got in, Kate." He held her gaze as he showed her the glass cutter in his hand. "But it's all right. I'm almost finished and I like it better this way."

She couldn't move. She stared at him, mesmerized.

"You might as well let me in. You can't stop me."

She jerked the drapes shut, closing him out.

Barricading herself inside with only a fragment of glass, a scrap of material . . .

She heard the sound of blade on glass.

She backed away from the window, stumbled on the hassock, almost fell, righted herself.

Oh God. Where was that policeman? The porch light was out, but surely he could see Ishmaru.

Maybe the policeman wasn't there.

And your husband never mentioned bribery in the ranks?

The drapes were moving.

He'd cut the window.

"Phyliss!" She ran down the hall. "Wake up." She threw open Joshua's door, flew across the room, and jerked him out of bed.

"Mom?"

"Shh, be very quiet. Just do what I tell you, okay?"

"What's wrong?" Phyliss was standing in the doorway. "Is Joshua sick?"

"I want you to leave here." She pushed Joshua toward her. "There's someone outside." She hoped he was still outside. Christ, he could be in the living room by now. "I want you to take Joshua out the back door and over to the Brocklemans'."

Phyliss instantly took Joshua's hand and moved toward the kitchen door. "What about you?"

She heard a sound in the living room. "*Go.* I'll be right behind you."

Phyliss and Joshua flew out the back door.

"Are you waiting for me, Kate?"

He sounded so close, too close. Phyliss and Joshua could not have reached the fence yet. No time to run. Stop him.

She saw him, a shadow in the doorway leading to the hall.

Where was the gun?

In her handbag on the living room table. She couldn't get past him. She backed toward the stove.

Phyliss usually left a frying pan out to cook breakfast in the morning. . . .

"I told you I was coming in. No one can stop me tonight. I had a sign."

She didn't see a weapon but the darkness was lit only by moonlight streaming through the window.

"Give up, Kate."

Her hand closed on the handle of the frying pan. "Leave me *alone*." She leaped forward and struck out at his head with all her strength.

He moved too fast but she connected with a glancing blow.

He was falling. . . .

She streaked past him down the hall. Get to the purse, the gun.

She heard him behind her.

She snatched up the handbag, lunged for the door, and threw the bolt.

Get to the policeman in the black-and-white.

She fumbled with the catch on her purse as she streaked down the driveway toward the black-and-white. Her hand closed on the gun and she threw the purse aside.

"He's not there, Kate," Ishmaru said behind her. "It's just the two of us."

"Susan Johnson's love scenes sparkle, sizzle, and burn!" —*Affaire de Coeur*

Through eleven nationally bestselling books, award winner Susan Johnson has won a legion of fans for her lushly romantic historical novels. Now she delivers her most thrilling tale yet—a searing blend of rousing adventure and wild, forbidden love . . .

TABOO

by Susan Johnson

Married against her will to the brutal Russian general who conquered her people, Countess Teo Korsakova has never known what it means to want a man . . . until now. Trapped behind enemy lines, held captive by her husband's most formidable foe, she should fear for her life. But all Teo feels in General Andre Duras's shattering presence is breathless passion. France's most victorious commander, Andre knows that he should do the honorable thing, knows too that on the eve of battle he cannot afford so luscious a distraction. Yet something about Teo lures him to do the unthinkable: to seduce his enemy's wife, and to let himself love a woman who can never be his.

He played chess the way he approached warfare, moving quickly, decisively, always on the attack. But she held her own, although her style was less aggressive, and when he took her first knight after long contention for its position, he said, "If your husband's half as good as you, he'll be a formidable opponent."

"I'm not sure you fight the same way."

"You've seen him in battle?"

"On a small scale. Against my grandfather in Siberia."

"And yet you married him?"

"Not by choice. The Russians traditionally take hostages from their conquered tribes. I'm the Siberian version. My clan sends my husband tribute in gold each year. So you see why I'm valuable to him."

"Not for gold alone, I'm sure," he said, beginning to move his rook.

"How gallant, Andre," she playfully declared.

His gaze came up at the sound of his name, his rook poised over the board, and their glances held for a moment. The fire crackled noisily in the hearth, the ticking of the clock sounded loud in the stillness, the air suddenly took on a charged hush, and then the general smiled—a smooth, charming smile. "You're going to lose your bishop, Teo."

She couldn't answer as suavely because her breath was caught in her throat and it took her a second to overcome the strange, heated feeling inundating her senses.

His gaze slid down her blushing cheeks and throat to rest briefly on her taut nipples visible through her white cashmere robe and he wondered what was happening to him that so demure a sight had such a staggering effect on his libido. He dropped his rook precipitously into place, inhaled, and leaned back in his chair, as if putting distance between himself and such tremulous innocence would suffice to restore his reason.

"Your move," he gruffly said.

"Maybe we shouldn't play anymore."

"Your move." It was his soft voice of command.

"I don't take orders."

"I'd appreciate it if you'd move."

"I'm not sure I know what I'm doing anymore." He lounged across from her, tall, lean, powerful, with predatory eyes, the softest of voices, and the capacity to make her tremble.

"It's only a game."

"This, you mean."

"Of course. What else would I mean?"

"I was married when I was fifteen, after two years of refinement at the Smolny Institute for Noble Girls," she pertinently said, wanting him to know.

"And you're very refined," he urbanely replied, wondering how much she knew of love after thirteen faithful years in a forced marriage. His eyes drifted downward again, his thoughts no longer of chess.

"My husband's not refined at all."

"Many Russians aren't." He could feel his erection begin to rise, the thought of showing her another side of passionate desire ruinous to his self-restraint.

"It's getting late," she murmured, her voice quavering slightly.

"I'll see you upstairs," he softly said.

When he stood, his desire was obvious; the form-fitting regimentals molded his body like a second skin.

Gripping the chair arms, she said, "No," her voice no more than a whisper.

He moved around the small table and touched her then because he couldn't help himself, because she was quivering with desire like some virginal young girl and the intoxicating image of such tremulous need was more carnal than anything he'd ever experienced. His hand fell lightly on her shoulder, its heat tantalizing, tempting.

She looked up at him and, lifting her mouth to his, heard herself say, "Kiss me."

"Take my hand," he murmured. And when she did, he pulled her to her feet and drew her close so the scent of her was in his nostrils and the warmth of her body touched his.

"Give me a child." Some inner voice prompted the words she'd only dreamed for years.

"No," he calmly said, as if she hadn't asked the unthinkable from a stranger, and then his mouth covered hers and she sighed against his lips. And as their kiss deepened and heated their blood and drove away reason, they both felt an indefinable bliss—torrid and languorous, heartfelt and, most strangely—hopeful in two people who had long ago become disenchanted with hope.

And then her maid's voice drifted down the stairway, the intonation of her native tongue without inflection. "He'll kill you," she declared.

Duras's mouth lifted and his head turned to the sound. "What did she say?"

"She reminded me of the consequences."

"Which are?"

"My husband's wrath."

He was a hairsbreadth from selfishly saying, *Don't worry*, but her body had gone rigid in his arms at her maid's pointed admonition and at base he knew better. He knew he wouldn't be there to protect her from her husband's anger and he knew too that she was much too innocent for a casual night of love.

"Tamyr is my voice of reason."

He released her and took a step away, as if he couldn't trust himself to so benignly relinquish such powerful feeling. "We all need a voice of reason," he neutrally said. "Thank you for the game of chess."

"I'm sorry."

"Not more sorry than I," Duras said with a brief smile.

"Will I see you again?" She couldn't help herself from asking.

"Certainly." He took another step back, his need for her almost overwhelming. "And if you wish for anything during your stay with us, feel free to call on Bonnay."

"Can't I call on you?"

"My schedule's frenzied and, more precisely, your maid's voice may not be able to curtail me a second time."

"I see."

"Forgive my bluntness."

"Forgiven," she gently said.

"Good night, Madame Countess." He bowed with grace.

"Good night, Andre."

"Under other circumstances . . ." he began, and then shrugged away useless explanation.

"I know," she softly said. "Thank you."

He left precipitously, retreat uncommon for France's bravest general, but he wasn't sure he could trust himself to act the gentleman if he stayed.

"Michelle Martin writes fresh, funny, fast-paced contemporary romance with a delicious hint of suspense."
—Teresa Medeiros, nationally bestselling author of *Touch of Enchantment*

The irresistible Michelle Martin, author of *Stolen Hearts*, whips up a delectable new concoction of a woman chasing a dream . . . and the man who fulfills her sweetest fantasies . . .

STOLEN MOMENTS

by Michelle Martin

It was just after midnight when the Princess of Pop made her escape, leaving behind the syrupy-sweet ballads and the tyrannical manager who had made her famous. All Harley Jane Miller wanted was a vacation: two weeks on her own in New York before recording her next album. Yet now that she's tasted freedom, the Princess of Pop's gone electric: changing her clothes, her music, and her good-girl image. And she's never going back. Harley knows it will take some quick thinking to shake her greedy manager. But she never suspects she'll be waylaid by a diamond heist, the French mafia, and a devastatingly gorgeous detective who's determined to bring her in—by way of his bedroom . . . and when he does, Harley Jane will be more than willing to comply . . .

"Hello again, Miss Miller."
Harley's heart stopped. There was a roaring in her

ears. Slowly she turned her head and looked up. A man stood beside her bench. It was the hunk from Manny's, and he knew who she was. Staring up into those dark eyes, she knew it was futile for her to even attempt to pretend that she didn't know that he knew who she was. "Are you Duncan Lang, the man who was asking questions about me at the RIHGA yesterday?"

"One and the same."

"Did Boyd send you?"

"Boyd *hired* me. I found you thanks to high technology and brilliant deductive reasoning."

Harley stared up at him. "Can you be bought off?"

His dark eyes crinkled in amusement. " 'Fraid not. Dad would be peeved. Colangco has a sterling reputation for honesty and results. Sorry," he said as he picked up her Maxi-Mouse. "Shall we head back to the Hilton for your things?"

Crud, he knew where she was staying. Harley tried to think, but her brain felt like iced sludge. It was over. She hadn't even had two full days of freedom yet, and it was over.

Her chest ached. "I'm twenty-six, a grown woman, legally independent," she stated. "You can't just haul me back to Boyd like he *owns* me!"

"I can when that's what I'm hired to do."

"But I haven't even had a chance to try out my new guitar," Harley said, hot tears welling in her eyes. She hurriedly pushed them back. "Boyd is not about to let me keep it. He hates electric guitars. He doesn't think they're feminine."

"What?"

"And he won't let me wear black clothes, or red

clothes, or anything resembling a bright color. And no jeans. Not even slacks."

"He's got a tight rein on you," Duncan Lang agreed as he sat down beside her.

"He is sucking the life's blood out of me."

"Why do you let him?"

"Boyd is deaf to anyone's 'no' except his own," Harley replied bitterly.

"But as you pointed out, you are twenty-six and legally independent. You don't have to put up with his crap if you don't want to."

"Why do you care?" Harley demanded, glaring up at the treacherous hunk.

"I don't," Duncan Lang stated. "I'm just curious. You did a very good job of hiding yourself among eight million people—"

"*You* found me."

"Ah, well," he said, ducking his head in false modesty, "I'm a trained investigator, after all." His winsome smile must have charmed every female who'd even glanced at him sideways from the time he was sixteen. It made Harley's teeth grate. "My point is that," he continued, "Boyd's opinion notwithstanding, you seem fully capable of taking care of yourself. Fire the control freak and get on with your life."

"It's not that easy," Harley said, her arms tightening around the guitar case. "I owe everything to Boyd: my career, my success, my fame, my money. I'd still be a little hick from Oklahoma if it weren't for him. And I'm not so sure I can make it in the industry without him now."

"He *has* run a number on you, hasn't he?"

"Oh yeah," Harley said, staring down at the concrete ground.

"So why did you run away?"

Harley felt her stomach freeze over. Her jaws began to liquefy. She stared blindly at the fountain. "The music stopped coming," she whispered.

"I thought so," Duncan Lang said.

Harley turned her head and met his sympathetic black gaze. It nearly undid her. Oh God, her music! "It's been two months and not a note, not a lyric." The well she had depended on all of her life had gone dry. There was nothing left to be tapped. She looked up at him, pleading for a stay of execution. "I thought if I could just have a few weeks of fun. A few weeks of not being Jane Miller. A few weeks of just letting go, and maybe it would come back. Maybe I'd be okay again. Then I'd fly to L.A., get back on the treadmill, and make the damn album for Sony."

Harley almost clapped a hand to her mouth. Years ago Boyd had forbidden Jane Miller to swear in public or private.

"A reasonable plan," Lang agreed.

"Then let me go!" Harley said, her hand clutching his arm. "Let me have my two weeks. No one will be hurt. I'll come back and fulfill all of my obligations, I promise."

"Sorry, Princess, that's not part of the plan."

"Who the *hell* do you think you are?" Harley exploded. "You're not God. You have no right to tell me where to go or what to do. I'll fly off to *Brazil* if I feel like it and you can't stop me."

"Oh yes I can," he retorted.

"How?"

"By physical force if necessary."

He looked like he could do it too. "*Oh*, I hate men," Harley seethed. "The arrogance. The stupidity."

"I'm actually pretty intelligent," Duncan Lang retorted, dark eyes glittering. "Don't forget, I found you."

"If you found me, you can lose me."

"No."

"Dammit, Lang—"

"I signed a contract, Princess. I am obligated to fulfill it."

"But not today," Harley pleaded. "You don't have to fulfill it today, or tomorrow, or even a week from tomorrow. Give me back my holiday, Mr. Lang."

He looked down at her. A gamine with breasts, dressed all in black. He'd known an odd kind of fascination as he'd surreptitiously watched her in Manny's Music. She had a quality . . . like Sleeping Beauty just waking up from a hundred years' sleep and discovering the world anew.

He'd never felt that kind of immediate attraction to a woman in his life. Oh sure, he'd been drawn to beautiful women, and voluptuous women, and even bewitching women. Harley was none of those things. She was just somehow . . . familiar.

"Okay, Princess, here's the deal," he said with sudden decision. "I'll do a little digging while you make like a tourist or a musician or whatever the hell it is you want to be today. But at midnight I put you back in your pumpkin and return you to Mr. Monroe." Duncan held out his hand. "Deal?"

Faux brown eyes stared up at him a moment. Then Harley Jane Miller's slim fingers slid across his hand, clasping it firmly, disconcerting him with a sudden feeling of connection. "Deal."

DON'T MISS THESE FABULOUS
BANTAM WOMEN'S FICTION TITLES

On Sale in November

LONG AFTER MIDNIGHT
by Iris Johansen
New York Times *bestselling author of* The Ugly Duckling

A gifted scientist awakens to a nightmare when she realizes she is a ruthless killer's target. The medical research to which she has devoted her life could get her killed and her only hope is to make that medical breakthrough and elude her enemy until she can destroy him.   ___57181-8 $6.99/$8.99

TABOO
by nationally bestselling author Susan Johnson

When the wife of a Russian officer finds herself on the wrong side of the line, her care is assigned to Napoleon's most formidable general. And in a politically torn Europe, the two find they must choose between conflicting loyalties and a glorious forbidden passion.   ___57215-6 $5.99/$7.99

STOLEN MOMENTS
by the irresistible Michelle Martin, author of Stolen Hearts

To the world she is the Princess of Pop, but what Harley Miller wants is some time out of the limelight. What she gets is trouble: a diamond heist, the French mafia, and a devastatingly gorgeous detective. Now he's determined to bring her in—by way of his bedroom, and soon all she can think about is being with him . . . if only for a few stolen moments.   ___57649-6 $5.50/$7.50

TIDINGS OF GREAT JOY
by New York Times *bestselling author Sandra Brown*

Ria and Taylor's night of unexpected passion led to a quickie wedding in order to legitimize the baby Ria carried. The plan was to divorce after the birth. But when Taylor makes it clear he is taking her for his wife—in every way—their Christmas miracle may just be true love.   ___10403-9 $17.95/$24.95

Ask for these books at your local bookstore or use this page to order.

Please send me the books I have checked above. I am enclosing $____ (add $2.50 to cover postage and handling). Send check or money order, no cash or C.O.D.'s, please.

Name _____

Address _____

City/State/Zip _____

Send order to: Bantam Books, Dept. FN158, 2451 S. Wolf Rd., Des Plaines, IL 60018
Allow four to six weeks for delivery.

Prices and availability subject to change without notice.   FN 158 11/97